A. Gringo

Through the Land of the Aztecs

A. Gringo

Through the Land of the Aztecs

ISBN/EAN: 9783742819871

Manufactured in Europe, USA, Canada, Australia, Japa

Cover: Foto ©Andreas Hilbeck / pixelio.de

Manufactured and distributed by brebook publishing software
(www.brebook.com)

A. Gringo

Through the Land of the Aztecs

THROUGH

THE

LAND OF THE AZTECS

OR

LIFE AND TRAVEL IN MEXICO

BY

A GRINGO

LONDON

SAMPSON LOW, MARSTON & COMPANY

LIMITED)

St. Dunstan's House

FETTER LANE, FLEET STREET, E.C.

1892

PREFACE

MEXICO is rapidly taking a prominent place as an object of interest both to men of business and to travellers. The former are becoming fully alive to the immense advantages it possesses for the investment of capital, whilst the latter are beginning to appreciate its grand scenery and its historical associations.

The continued peace, and security to life and property which it has so long enjoyed under the wise rule of Don Porfirio Diaz, who is offering every inducement to foreign enterprise, have made financiers eager to assist in the development of its resources. Its wonderful ruins, the invigorating air of its high table-land, and the balmy atmosphere of the Tropics around its quaint and picturesque old cities, are attracting numerous visitors from all parts of the world.

Those valuable aids to British enterprise, the Consular Reports, have furnished copious and exhaustive statistics of Mexico; antiquarians have published the results of their labours ; but my object is simply to give a plain account of several years' experience in the country, to show its recent progress, and to enable the reader to judge of its future. Social and business intercourse with many of its leading men, as well as prolonged periods of travel over the greater part of its territory, by rail, stage-coach and steamer, on horseback and in canoes, have afforded me exceptional facilities for studying the country and all classes of the people.

A fear lest my literary powers may fail to satisfy the critics, so much dreaded by the inexperienced author, has constrained me, as a slight protection, to send forth this book under the veil of a pseudonym. If I incur the ire of any exacting reviewer, I shall at least have the satisfaction of feeling that my friends will never know that I am the particular ' Gringo ' upon whom the bolt has fallen.   On the other hand, I shall feel amply repaid should I be successful in interesting my readers in a sunny land, in which I have spent so many happy hours, and where I have received so much courtesy from its inhabitants.

Perhaps I ought to mention that the word ' Gringo,' the origin of which is explained in the course of my narrative, is applied equally to English and American visitors by Mexican natives.

CONTENTS

CHAPTER I

CHAPTER II

CHAPTER III

CHAPTER IV

CHAPTER XI

CHAPTER XII

CHAPTER XIII

CHAPTER XIV

CHAPTER XV

CHAPTER XVI

CHAPTER XVII

ILLUSTRATIONS

THROUGH

THE

LAND OF THE AZTECS

CHAPTER I

Arrival off Vera Cruz—Origin of the word 'Gringo'—Vera Cruz
by night—Yellow Jack—Zopilotes—Its commerce, harbour and
probable future—Northers—San Juan de Ulloa—Journey to
Mexico City.

AFTER a delightful voyage from New York in the
'City of Alexandria,' we arrived in Vera Cruz in
October 1883.

This is the only pretence of a harbour on the
Gulf side into which ships of average draught can
enter, while Nature has given the country several
excellent ports on the Pacific Coast. The entrance
is dangerous and can only be attempted by daylight,
a low reef of coral forming the harbour, which is
guarded by the fort of San Juan de Ulloa, now used
as a prison for political and criminal offenders.

Very beautiful did Vera Cruz look as it lay along

B

the shore, flanked on each side by a narrow belt of yellow sand, bathed in the rays of the morning sun, with a background of cocoanut-trees waving in the breeze and a dense tropical vegetation. In the distance were the blue mountains of the Sierra Madre and the snow-tipped peak of Orizaba, like a gigantic sugar-loaf. The cupolas of the churches dazzled the eye with the reflection of the sun's rays on their tile-covered domes ; and the low one-storeyed houses, with their white walls and green verandahs, looked invitingly cool. Behind us frowned the grim old fortress ; while beyond, stretching to a cloudless horizon, was the gently heaving surface of the ocean, which separated us from the dear ones at home. As we swung round to our moorings we could see boats of all descriptions putting out to meet us, from the neat white Government gig to the lighter, heeling over under her big lateen sail, on her way to deliver our good ship of its cargo. After the arrival of the health officers, who were duly satisfied with our bill of health, and after bidding farewell to the courteous officers of the steamer, we took boat for the shore, not without lengthy bargaining with the owner, who was keenly alive to the necessity of making the utmost out of the freshly arrived ' Gringos.' This word is said to have had its origin during the American war, when some American soldiers were heard singing ' Green grow the Rushes, Oh ! ' From the first two words the natives made the nickname ' Gringo,' which has stuck to the Americans and English ever since.

A few minutes' sail brought us to the Mole, where crowds of gesticulating negroes and native porters awaited us, clamouring for our patronage. As I had taken the precaution of arranging with our boatman for the delivery of our luggage at the hotel, we were spared further extortion.

The inspection at the Custom House occupied some time, for we had a considerable quantity of baggage; but the officials were very polite and the examination was not so vexatious as we had feared it would be. However, we congratulated ourselves prematurely on the ease with which we had introduced sundry little luxuries without payment of duty, as our experience in Mexico City proved later on.

We now directed our steps to the Hotel Mexico, opposite the Custom House. After mounting many stairs, and traversing passages, the floors of which consisted of iron gratings that ventilated the whole building, we were shown into a small room with wooden partitions, commanding a glorious view of the sea and harbour. It contained two little truck beds, clean, and covered with muslin mosquito nets that prepared us for coming trials at night. We comforted ourselves with the reflection that it would only be for that night, and went downstairs to partake of our first Mexican meal. Although there were too many stews for the English taste, it was not such a bad meal. The fish was delicious; a good bottle of claret, for which only 75 cents was charged, and some fruit, completed the repast.

Who said Vera Cruz was hot? It is true that out there on the Custom House Square the sunshine was dazzling; but the sea-breeze, that circulated freely through our little restaurant, was delightfully cool.

But when we went out the heat was blinding and scorching. We were soon bathed in perspiration, and could realise what a Mexican tropical sun could do when he put his shoulder to the wheel. A few minutes' stroll was quite enough, and we were glad to get back to the hotel to cool off and get a siesta. The beds were hard, but we were soon enjoying a pleasant nap.

After dinner we again sallied forth; and now, in the cool of the evening, we found an animated scene, where, before, the whole town had appeared deserted. The pretty little plaza was filled with people strolling around, or sitting on the stone seats, chatting gaily and enjoying the strains of the regimental band. Under the 'portales,' or arcades, so dear to the Mexican, and especially to the Vera Cruzan, were seated little groups of men, enjoying sundry drinks, with their chairs tilted against the pillars, discussing the topics of the day in Spanish, English, French, and German. Burly sea-captains, substantial-looking merchants, and dandified young men in alpaca coats and white duck trousers were consuming Bass, mint julep, brandies and sodas, cocktails and refrescos, according to their national tastes, and evidently enjoying their evening thoroughly after the heat and burden of the day.

How picturesque the square looked, with its cocoanut and other trees, through the thick foliage of which glanced the rays of the electric light on to the flashing fountains, pretty gardens, and marble pavement, and the groups of young men and maidens laughing and ogling, in spite of ever-present relatives and duennas! Fanned by the gentle sea-breeze, inhaling the perfumes of the tropical flowers, and listening to the dreamy music of the Danza, we sat enjoying that delightful feeling of *dolce far niente* which can only be experienced in its perfection in the Tropics. Later on, when silence fell on the deserted plaza, and the town was hushed, save for the occasional plash of the waves, how beautiful was the night! A cloudless, star-sprinkled sky, and a clear, full moon, that brought out sharply every line of the quaint old church, while two Turkey buzzards, perched on the lofty cross, stood out black against the snow-white stone.

'Birds of evil omen' said, next day, a nervous fellow-passenger, who had lodged for the night at the Hotel Diligencia, on the plaza. 'Fancy their daring to sully the holy cross with their foul presence! I could hardly sleep for watching the hideous creatures, and from the bottom of my heart I wish myself out of this fever-stricken hole.'

It is sad to think that here have perished so many thousands from that dreadful scourge the 'Yellow Jack.' How many young hearts, bright with hope and brave spirits, and coming from afar to seek their fortune in this distant land, stricken down in the bloom of youth and manhood, lie still for ever in that white cemetery yonder! The year before we reached Vera Cruz there had been a fearful outbreak, which roused the authorities at last. By breaking down the old walls, extending the area of the population, and giving proper attention to the hygiene of the city, Vera Cruz has been made practically free from yellow fever.

One of the quaintest sights in Vera Cruz is the number of zopilotes, as the Turkey buzzards are called, which perform the duty of town scavengers, and are protected by law, a fine being exacted for killing any of these useful birds. But it is a repugnant spectacle to watch them sweep down on the scavenger's cart; whenever it stops it becomes at once black with a struggling mass of zopilotes, fighting for the garbage it contains, and flying off with cries of disgust when it is put in motion.

The streets are picturesque, with their houses of white or light blue tints, green wooden verandahs, and gay sunblinds, behind which sit the dark-eyed señoritas at their needlework or gossiping.

At the time of our arrival there was hardly an

Englishman resident in the town; but now, with a branch of the English Bank, another railroad rapidly approaching completion, and the petroleum refinery works, there are a good many English and Americans, and a very pleasant genial little colony it is. The principal foreign population is German, and there are a good many French and Spanish, all engaged in commerce.

Now that it has lost its unsavoury reputation for yellow fever, it is the favourite resort of the wealthier inhabitants of the capital, who fill the streets to overflowing during the winter months, when the climate is delightful. But the Vera Cruzans have a horror of the rarefied atmosphere of the tableland, and they will never stop in Mexico City a day longer than they can help.

There are many old-established wealthy firms in the town, and, in spite of the threatened rivalry of Tampico, the Vera Cruz merchants do not seem to have much fear for the future of their port. There is a good deal of commercial activity at present, but there can be no doubt that the importance of Vera Cruz will be very seriously threatened when Tampico can offer vessels a fair harbour.

The measures to improve the Vera Cruz harbour by building a sea-wall to the north are being executed in a very dilatory, haphazard manner, and unless something is done, and that soon, to make a safe place of anchorage, it is not difficult to foretell its future.

For years past labourers have been dropping huge blocks of concrete into the sea, to form the sea-wall, but as the stones have been allowed to fall anywhere and anyhow, the result will certainly be money and labour uselessly spent.

In all probability the present port will be abandoned in favour of San Anton Lizardo, which lies a short distance down the coast, and offers far better anchorage. The great danger in the Vera Cruz port during a 'Norther' lies among the shipping itself, for steamers can hardly avoid colliding, there not being sufficient space to allow of their being properly handled should they break from their moorings. These Northers, which are the curse of the Gulf, from their sudden appearance and great fury, are of frequent occurrence between the months of October and May, working terrible havoc among sailing vessels. The steamships have always steam up in case of an emergency. I have been rowing in a perfect calm, with a clear sky overhead, and upon hearing the cry of 'Norte' among the sailors on the ships, I have just had time to scull ashore for dear life, and within five minutes there was a boiling sea, in which no lighter could have lived.

The effects of these gales are felt all along the coast, far into the interior, and even to the mountain ranges. On the plateau and over the whole Gulf side a marked change of temperature occurs with the advent of a Norther; the air is often cold, and accompanied by a penetrating drizzle. The Norther is of advantage, however, inasmuch as it clears the atmosphere of mosquitoes and all germs of disease. Yellow fever is unknown during the months in which it blows; and the sudden change from a sunny climate to cold and damp, though trying, is not prejudicial to health beyond causing catarrhs.

When in Vera Cruz, on another occasion, I visited 'San Juan de Ulloa,' and was shown by the Governor over that part of the dungeons set apart for criminals, entrance to the apartments in which political prisoners are confined being forbidden. This is a terrible place in which to expiate a crime; and the convict's life must be an exceptionally hard one. In one great cavernous cell were confined some hundreds of prisoners at the time of my visit. They were formed into a double line, every fourth man holding aloft a small oil-lamp. When the eye became accustomed to the gloom the figures of the wretched men could be discerned stripped to the waist, with gloomy, ferocious faces, to which the flickering lights gave an uncanny aspect. Those faces have often haunted me; not one of them but was evil, no signs of shame or of repentance were visible, and one could not help feeling that it was well that such men should be kept in confinement for the benefit of humanity at large. The prisoners take it in turn to work on the rocks surrounding the fortress, carrying coal to the lighters under the fierce rays of the tropical sun. One or

two were confined in a separate cell, and I was told
that these had committed so many grave offences that
they had been confined for life without further trial.
In their spare moments the convicts carve cocoanut-
shells with sharp-pointed nails, which they fit into
rough wood handles, no knives being allowed.   Many
of these shells are worked into artistic patterns, and
on all is the pathetic motto, 'Recuerdo de San Juan
de Ulloa,'[1] to remind the purchaser, in his happy
freedom, of the prisoners who have spent over these
shells so many hours of labour.   Pieces of beautiful
white coral may also be bought, but they are very
brittle.

The day after our arrival in Vera Cruz we were
up betimes, for our train left for Mexico at 5 A.M.
The cars of the Mexican railway are built after the
American fashion, and are fairly comfortable, the
train being drawn by huge Fairleigh engines of
the most powerful class, to enable it to climb the
steep grades on the road.   There is no better built
line in the world, and it is kept in admirable order,
accidents being of rare occurrence.

The scenery traversed is said to be the grandest
and most beautiful on earth, and it is a difficult task
to do it justice.

Leaving the sandy waste that surrounds Vera
Cruz, we soon entered a region of tropical vegetation,
and for many miles the road lay through a tangled

[1] 'Souvenir of San Juan de Ulloa.'

mass of trees and shrubs, entirely covered with wild convolvulus and other creepers, which gave them sometimes the weirdest of forms. Nowhere, I think, is the morning air so deliciously balmy as in the Tropics; certainly this morning was no exception to the rule. The heat, which was already beginning to make itself felt, was tempered by the sea-breeze. We stopped at pretty little stations, with houses embowered in a wreath of flowers and shaded by waving banana-trees, and began the gradual ascent which was to bring us to the high tableland. Soon we reached Cordoba, the great coffee-growing district, and here we were assailed by a crowd of Indian women and children, offering bananas, pineapples, and all sorts of tropical fruits and flowers for sale. Fancy a basket of pineapples for twenty-five cents! I calculated that they cost about three halfpence apiece. Everybody bought; the car was redolent with the odour of fruit and flowers; and, for awhile, even the Mexicans ceased their endless chatter in the enjoyment of the rich, ripe fruit.

After passing through apparently endless groves of coffee-trees with their dark glossy foliage, the scenery became wilder and grander. Away in the distance we caught a glimpse of Orizaba rearing its cone-shaped, snow-clad peak to the high heaven; and a short run through the Valley of Orizaba brought us to the town of the same name. After a stop here we were again on the move, and as the train rolled out of the station we could distinguish the quaint old church and white houses of this picturesque little town lying at the foot of high mountains, whose tops were hidden among the misty clouds, and surrounded by plantations through which ran pretty lanes lined with banana-trees.

The scenery now became inexpressibly grand, and the eye was never tired of watching the varied landscape lying far below, and viewed from the edge of precipices which made one shudder to think of the consequences of an accident. High above us was to be seen the road, winding along the sides of the mountains. Almost at the summit of one we saw a little white speck, and could hardly believe that it was one of the stations of the line, and that our engine could ever drag the heavy train to such a height. Sometimes we were carried along the side of a torrent rushing far below us, or skirted a ravine with the road running parallel on the other side, to reach which we crossed a magnificent iron bridge in a horsehoe form ; at other times plunging into tunnels and cuttings, hewn from the solid rock, to emerge into fresh scenes of beauty. As the grade became steeper we became aware of the rarefied atmosphere by the quickened action of our lungs. The air grew chilly, and by the time we had reached the highest point on the line, nearly 10,000 feet above sea-level, we should have been glad of warmer clothing. Then began the gradual descent into the tableland. The dry, dusty plains, enlivened only by the monotonous rows of maguey plants, which seem to stretch away to the foot of the mountains, took the place of the luxuriant tropical vegetation we had left behind only a short time since. The air again became warm, but with a sultry, feverish heat which seemed to dry up the pores of the skin, a process exceedingly unpleasant to the subject, and very materially aided by the cloud of fine dust which, despite every precaution, penetrated the car. As the sun sank into the horizon we were glad to think that our journey was nearly at an end. Soon afterwards the train slowly rolled into the station, and we were in the city of Mexico.

CHAPTER II

The city by night—The Custom House—Situation, climate, and seasons of Mexico—The lakes—Mexico's smells—Prevalent diseases—Suitability of the climate for consumptives.

ON asking for our luggage we were informed that it must pass through the Custom House, which would not be open till the next day. We wore only light clothing suitable for the Tropics, but there was no help for it; so, having secured a hearse-like coach, we were driven to the Hotel Gillow, of which we had read so much in a book on Mexico, then recently published. We were given an interior room, looking on to the patio, barely furnished, and very cold, for the sun never fell on that side of the house. Opposite to the hotel was the principal restaurant of the city, the Concordia. There we supped, and then strolled out to endeavour to form some idea of our new place of residence. It was a melancholy walk, for, though hardly 8 P.M., the streets were deserted, the shops all closed, and no lights were to be seen nor music heard in the closely-shuttered houses. Accustomed to the gay evening outdoor life of Southern Spain, and fresh from the pleasant evening in Vera Cruz, this was quite a disenchantment, and very soon, finding the air chilly and penetrating, we were glad to return to our hotel. The following morning our troubles with the Custom House of Mexico City began. All goods imported into the country must, after examination at the port of entry, suffer another inspection at their ultimate destination, causing much needless annoyance and trouble. This time our baggage was subject to a minute scrutiny. For hours I stood in the hot sun opening and closing boxes and portmanteaux, perspiring at every pore, and struggling to keep my temper, while the lynx-eyed inspector carefully examined their contents. Apparently my politeness had little effect, for he deliberately set aside first one article and then another as dutiable, until my hair stood on end at the duties I should have to pay. When the examination was concluded he coolly told me to pack everything up again. After all no duty was payable, and he had probably been actuated by a desire to annoy me. I afterwards learned that if I had left the matter in the hands of the baggage-express people I might have been spared my trouble, the Custom House officials always being suspicious when the owner of the baggage clears it himself.

Mexico City is situated in a fertile valley, surrounded by mountains, and enjoying a climate which, in the opinion of those who have travelled over the world, is considered unrivalled. Its great altitude, over 7,000 feet above sea-level, accounts for its moderate temperature, the cool breezes from the mountains counteracting the heat of the sun. The thermometer does not vary more than from 70 degrees to 80 degrees in the shade, and the summer, which is often so trying in the United States and in Europe, is delightfully cool.

The seasons are divided into the dry and rainy, the former commencing in November and lasting till the following June. During this time of the year no rain falls, with the exception of perhaps a few heavy showers in March or April. From morn to night the sun shines in unclouded splendour. Occasionally a heavy Norther signals its approach with two or three cloudy, chilly days, the atmosphere being sometimes charged with mist. During such days all Mexico grumbles at the absence of its beloved sun, and with reason, for, during the short duration of the Norther, existence is not comfortable to the indolent, sun-loving natives. The evenings are somewhat cold, light overcoats and wraps being worn at this time during the winter. The rainy season is the most pleasant, for although rain falls daily, its duration is limited to one or two hours in the afternoon or evening. Old residents declare that a great change is noticeable now as compared with ten or twelve years back, when the showers fell with almost unbroken punctuality from 2 to 4 P.M. Now, days often pass without rain, which falls late at night. The mornings are delicious. It is then that Nature appears in all her glory, and the air becomes sweet and refreshing.

The vegetation is profuse, and the valley is one expanse of emerald green, broken here and there by the lakes. These lakes, Texcoco, Chalco, and Xochimilco, lie slightly above one another, thus constituting a danger of inundation, which the city has suffered from severely on one or two occasions. Once in the early history of the city it was flooded to a depth of seven feet. There being no outlet for the waters, the city remained submerged for years, and incalculable loss of life and property was the disastrous result. To avoid the risk of another catastrophe of this kind, the Spaniards commenced the Nochistongo Cut, a gigantic enterprise which cost the lives of many thousands of unfortunate slaves, but to this day remains unfinished. These lakes have decreased considerably in size, and do not now menace the city seriously, but their depth is always carefully watched during the rains.

The rarefied air allows the smells of the city to escape rapidly, otherwise Mexico, which certainly beats the famed Cologne in this respect, would have long ago been depopulated. The Mexicans say that they can tell the street they happen to be in blindfolded by its peculiar odours. But the stenches disappear at once in the thin air, and Mexico is to-day a fairly healthy city—a fact attested by the general good health of the foreigners and all those who lead

c

temperate and active lives. The death-rate, it is true, is high, but it must be remembered that the mortality exists among the poor, who lead such a miserable existence that they would have little chance of long life anywhere. Their food consists of nasty messes, of which offal and rotten meat often form part, and they live in hovels of the most filthy description.

The number of inhabitants was estimated at 300,000 many years ago; since then the city has developed considerably, and it is generally believed, by those who are in a position to speak with authority, that the present population is about 500,000.

The diseases most prevalent are small-pox, typhoid fever, and pneumonia. Cases of the latter frequently occur in the winter from exposure to the chilly night air. It is curious that the reason alleged for the entire absence of fire-places in the capital is the danger of going from a heated room into the cold air ; and it will take a long time to reconcile the inhabitants to artificial heating. I believe there is not a single open fireplace used in the whole city. A few American families have stoves in their rooms.

In spite of the risks incurred from sudden contact with the night air, it is the opinion of medical men that this is an excellent climate for people with weak lungs, particularly in the spring and summer months ; a little lower altitude being best suited for consumptive patients in the winter. I had a proof of the accuracy of this opinion in the case of a gentleman who arrived in Mexico with a hectic flush and a 'churchyard cough.' After a residence of a year in the country, spending the summer in the city and the winter on a hacienda in a somewhat warmer part of the interior, he became another man, and is now strong and healthy.

CHAPTER III

THE streets of Mexico present a curious spectacle to the foreigner, as he views the stream of human life which flows through them. Here is plainly visible the small proportion of the civilised to the uncivilised, of the wealthy to the starving. The quaint dresses and types that meet the eye in every direction increase the variety of the scene. The water-carrier, with that patient look often seen on the faces of those who carry heavy burdens, in a leather jacket, with his number conspicuous on a bright brass plate, cotton breeches, over which falls a leather apron, and a stout leather cap, with the broad strap round the forehead supporting the heavy jar that hangs at his back, looks very picturesque. The man carrying the offal from the slaughter-house for sale to the poor is a disgusting object. In filthy rags, smeared with blood from head to foot, he trudges along, carrying his load in a cone-shaped basket, the weight of which is

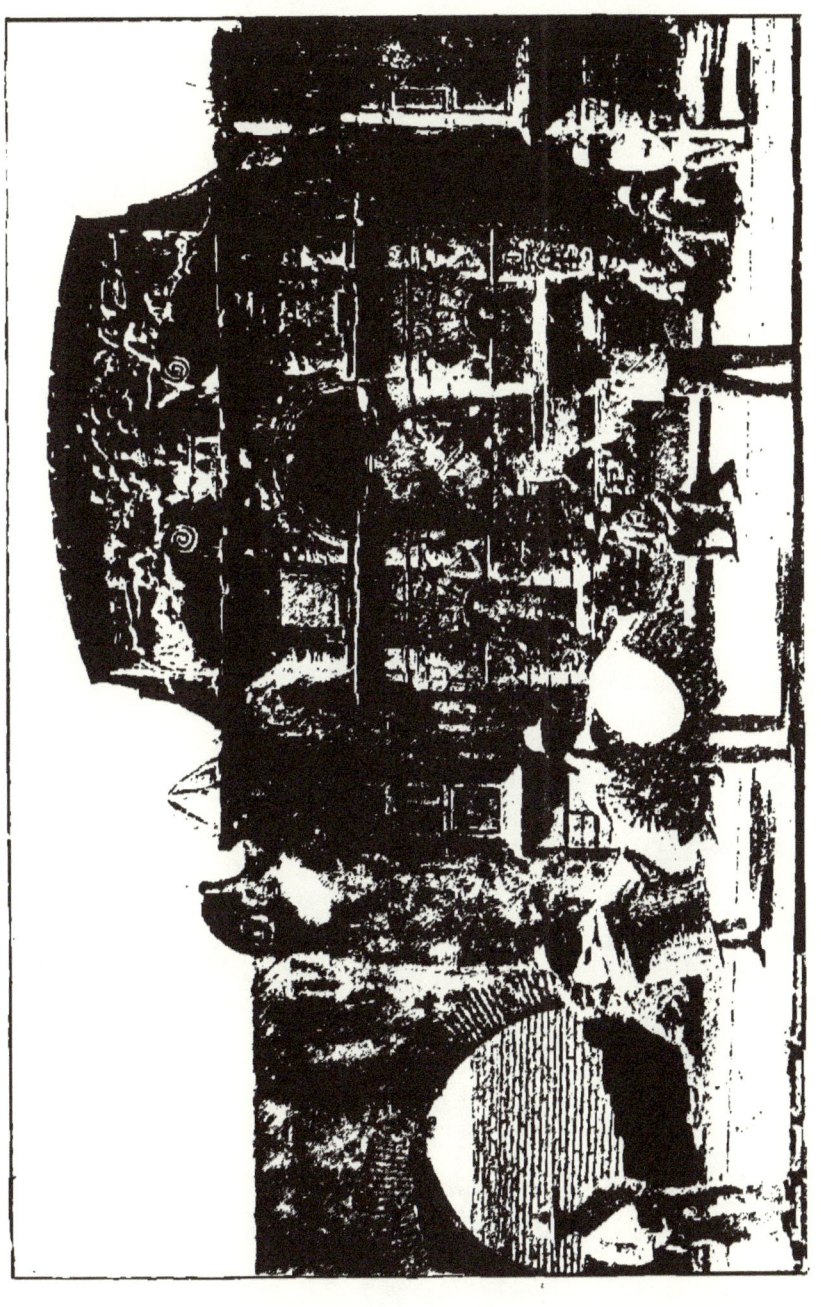

STREET SCENE, MEXICO

evident from the tension of the muscles of his bare legs. Foot passengers take care to avoid coming into contact with him, for he heeds not what dainty garments he may sully. The grimy Carboneros,[1] with their burdens of charcoal brought from a distance of many leagues; Indians carrying empty coffins on their heads; processions of Cargadores carrying pianos or wardrobes on their shoulders and smaller articles of furniture in the useful parihuelas;[2] trains of patient mules and donkeys bearing with stoical suffering the resounding whacks of the Arrieros[3] on their backs, covered with festering sores; handsome equipages drawn by spirited horses driven at a rapid rate through the crowded thoroughfare; natty policemen in blue clothes and white kepis standing at the corners. The pavement is crowded with fashionably-dressed dudes, hurrying clerks, dawdling Indians who get in everybody's way, ladies bent on shopping, ragged beggars, victims to every kind of horrible deformity, noisy lottery-ticket sellers—such, in outline, is the picture presented in the city streets.

Of all the working classes the most useful to the community are the Aguadores and Cargadores.[4] The former supply houses with water from the drinking-fountains, and are a numerous hard-working set of men; the latter are indispensable to life in Mexico. All picked men, honest and trustworthy, they deliver

---

[1] Coalmen.   [2] A species of small platform carried between two men.
[3] Mule drivers.   [4] Porters.

goods and collect the value, carry sacks of dollars to and from the banks, run errands, move furniture, and in the rainy season reap a harvest by carrying the foot-passengers across the flooded streets. They are to be seen at every corner of the principal streets, and a clap of the hands will bring half a dozen running. Their only fault is a love of horse-play while waiting for a job, the favourite pastime being to fight among themselves, using for weapons the heavy pads with which they protect the shoulders when carrying loads. These pads they swing at each other with little care for the passers-by, and now and then a gentleman or even a lady is knocked down, with, perhaps, serious injury, for they are powerful men and exert their full strength in the blows they deliver.

Here and there in the side streets we hear the sound of patting the hands, and know that a tortilla-house is not far off. In a grimy, foul-smelling room squat a number of women in tattered, dirty garments, grinding the maize; others, on their knees, are making the cakes, while at the charcoal fire stands the cook. The sight is enough to make one forswear tortillas for ever; but in the interior this is sometimes the only food to be obtained. The implements used are a flat, rough stone, which stands in a sloping position on three legs in front of the grinder, and a heavy metate held in the grinder's hands. Taking a handful of maize, the woman sprinkles it with water, mixed with a little lime, and grinds it with the metate to the bottom of the slab. She then replaces it at the top, and again moistens and grinds it, repeating the process until it has become a compact white paste. This she hands to the maker, who kneads it into a little round lump, which she pats between the palms of her dirty hands until it has become a round thin wafer. The cook then takes it, toasts it slightly on both sides, and the tortilla is ready to be eaten. There is a great knack in making tortillas, the 'light hand' so necessary for pastry at home being equally indispensable here. Families often keep a servant specially for making the tortillas, called a 'tortillera,' and she has her hands full at meal time, for she must serve each person at table with hot tortillas as fast as he can eat them. The poorest Mexican thinks it a hardship to eat a cold tortilla. And he is right, for it is as tough as shoe-leather. They only eat them cold when on a long journey or camping in the open, when they carry a sufficient stock to last them during their absence from home. When one has overcome the dislike of having his food prepared in this way, the tortillas are not so bad after all. They are tasteless, but satisfying, and, when accompanied by frisoles, fattening. They are used among the lower orders as a spoon to scoop up the food, which is swallowed with the piece of tortilla. It is considered bad manners to leave this impromptu spoon uneaten. This system of preparing the food has existed from time immemorial, and to-day the Mexican eats the tortillas made in the same way as in the times of his Aztec and Toltec forefathers.

The streets of Mexico City run due north and south, east and west, and present a picturesque medley of flat-roofed buildings, with green balconies and faded sunblinds, grated bow windows, and huge double doors. The houses, at some remote age, were painted in different colours, now faded considerably. All over those which have shops on the ground floor are painted advertisements, in huge letters, of the goods for sale. Here and there are to be seen fine old buildings in their original stone colour, a dark red, relieved by rich carvings, a pleasant contrast to the prevalent whitewash. There are some very handsome private buildings, one of the most notable among the old palaces being the Casa de Azulejos,[1] so-called because it is built of quaint-coloured glazed tiles. There is a legend that its owner vowed that he would build a house of tiles if they cost him a dollar apiece. On the completion of the house it was found that its actual cost exceeded what the tiles alone would have amounted to at the price named.

The finest of all the specimens of ancient architecture is the Hotel Iturbide. It was originally the palace of the emperor of that name, and is full of curious work. The stone gutters, that project far

[1] House of tiles.

from the roof, are carved into grotesque heads, and the walls of the patio are covered with curious stonework, while the richly gilt carving on one of the doors seems to denote that the room of which it forms the entrance must have been used as the imperial chapel. This large building, standing in the most central part of San Francisco Street, is the property of the Iturbe family, Mexican millionaires who occupy one of the handsomest palaces in Paris, and rarely visit their native land.

Another grand old house stands at the corner of Colisco and San Francisco Streets, opposite to the Hotel San Carlos. It was once the palace of a wealthy Mexican magnate, whose immense riches were obtained from his silver mines. Tradition says that, on the occasion of his daughter's marriage the enormous patio was paved with bars of silver, over which was driven the carriage bearing the bride from the paternal mansion. *Tempora mutantur!* The patio is now the storing-place of adjoining shops for their empty packing-cases, and the building itself is let out in viviendas,[1] while groceries and boot-shops occupy the ground floor.

The style of Mexican architecture, both in churches and houses, is almost invariably the same. The interiors of the latter are built around a square courtyard, the lower part of the building being used for porters' rooms, stabling, and offices, while the

[1] Flats.

upper portion is occupied by the family. The houses are mostly two storeys high in the city, those of one storey having generally, projecting from the roof, stone slabs, which are to form the balconies of the first floor when the owner has found sufficient funds to add another storey. The principle which appears to be followed in building is to get together sufficient money to purchase a piece of ground and commence building. When the walls are partly up, and the funds are exhausted, the owner is content to wait for some lucky event that will enable him to complete his house, or sell the unfinished portion at a profit.

Unfinished houses are often seen both in the city and the interior. The residences of the wealthy have two, and sometimes three, patios, one behind the other, and are of great depth. In these patios are to be seen the carriages of the owner, with the horses harnessed, standing during the greater part of the day ready for use at a moment's notice. This architectural style is almost identical with that of Spain ; but one misses the handsome marble pavement and pillars, pretty fountains, and the glimpse of the family seated in rocking-chairs under the shade of the thick canvas awnings, which gives the Spanish house such a delightfully cool and inviting aspect. The patios of the Mexican houses are of rough-hewn stone, in the centre of which is the drain, and the porteros seem to take pleasure in keeping them damp and dirty-looking by throwing over them any water

they wish to get rid of. This contributes considerably to the bad smells that sometimes issue from the
doorways, though the really good houses are always
clean and adorned with handsome shrubs. The
patios of some of the houses are adorned with paintings that are not always of much merit, but I have
seen one or two that are good. The mansion of
Mr. C. has at the back of the patio a well-executed
painting of a country scene, in the foreground of
which is a water-mill. The wheel of the pump by
which the house is supplied is so placed that when in
motion it represents the mill-wheel, the effect being
very realistic. But the best has been executed by a
Swede, who carries on the business of house decorator,
and is an artist of no mean merit. In a handsome
new house he has painted a representation of the
valley of Mexico, with the mountain Ixtaccihuatl in
the background, its snow-covered summit appearing
to glisten in the sunshine as it falls on the patio.
From the street the passer-by can imagine without
any difficulty that he sees the valley and mountain
beyond. The foreground is so perfect that it is hard
to believe that the maguey plants depicted are not
real, and the colouring of the whole is a perfect
representation of Nature under a Mexican sun. Above
the patio runs the corridor, full of flowers and birdcages, which give it a pretty aspect. This corridor is
always roofed, being the only means of communication
round the house, unless the kitchen and bedrooms be

traversed to reach the drawing-room. The ground-floors consequently get little, if any, sunshine, and, although they are often let out as viviendas or flats, there is a great prejudice against them on this account. They are considered unhealthy, not only owing to the damp, but also because the sewage of the city lies so near the surface. When the drainage has been completed this will be remedied.

It has always been a mystery why the Spaniards in rebuilding the city selected its old site, when they had the choice of so many healthy positions in the hills around. Possibly some reason existed similar to that given by a Spaniard who was once asked why the Escorial Palace of Spain had been built in the midst of such a dreary wilderness of stones. He replied that he supposed the reason lay in the stones required for building being so handy. The Spaniards were unfortunate in their choice of location for the principal towns of Mexico. Nearly all stand in flat valleys, with no fall for the drainage, and to this day no one has discovered why the particular spot was selected upon which Vera Cruz now stands, when San Anton Lizardo would have been much more suitable as a port.

Of public buildings Mexico has few to boast from an architectural point of view. The Post Office and Museum are commonplace buildings, undistinguishable from the rest of the street. The Art Gallery is a plain red structure, with a few medallions for ornament. The Palace, in which are the Government offices, is an unsightly edifice, which mars one side of the Zocalo with its monotony of whitewashed walls. The Monte de Piedad[1] is another barrack-like building, and the Hospicio de los Pobres[2] is a vast old convent, in a deplorable state of decay, which spoils the look of the street running from San Francisco Street to the Paseo.[3] But in this, as in everything else, Mexico is improving. The present façade of the Palace will soon be replaced by a handsome exterior, and there is some talk of the old Hospicio being pulled down to make way for an American hotel.

Chapultepec Palace occupies an eminence at the end of the Paseo, commanding a fine view of the whole city and valley. Built on a mass of basaltic rock, on portions of which are visible hieroglyphics, evidently of ancient origin, the approach to the Palace of the Moctezumas from the great iron entrance-gates is striking. From the city, looking up the fine avenue of the Paseo, in which the eye first rests on the handsome monuments of Columbus and Cuauhtemoc, Chapultepec, lit up by the rays of the morning's sun, is very beautiful. On the top of the Palace is a pretty garden, from which an enchanting view is gained. Part of the Palace is set apart for the military academy, where the sons of the best families receive their military education, and form a credit-

---

[1] National pawnbroking establishment.　　[2] Poorhouse.
[3] Promenade.

able corps of good-looking cadets. The remainder is occupied by the President, and a handsomer residence for the people's first magistrate could hardly be wished for. Behind, at the foot of the hill, there is a romantic wood of ancient cypress-trees, from which the Spanish moss hangs in graceful folds, offering enchanting vistas along the avenues that stretch in every direction. No pains have been taken to lay out the ground, and I like it best as it is. Though only three miles from the city, one can almost fancy oneself in a primeval forest, with the ferns and curious shrubs shaded by the grand old trees, whose tangled roots cross the path at every step, to bury themselves like serpents in the dense vegetation around. Under the shade of the largest of these trees, which is of giant growth, Moctezuma took council with his wise men upon affairs of State. Here too is Moctezuma's bath, which in these prosaic days supplies the city with drinking water. Near the romantic cypress-woods, which stand at the back of the Palace, and are much favoured as a holiday resort, is Molino del Rey, the scene of a battle during the American war, and since used as a Government foundry. In front of the Palace, and at the foot of the rock, is the handsome monument erected by their comrades to the memory of the Chapultepec cadets who fell in the American War, on which those of the present generation lay fresh flowers every morning.

The Paseo de la Reforma is the fashionable after-noon promenade, especially on Sundays and feast days, when all Mexico turns out. It is a beautiful drive, extending for a length of about two and a half miles, and fringed by a double avenue of trees, principally eucalyptus. On both sides is the fertile valley bounded by the mountain ranges, and on the left going towards Chapultepec are visible the mountains Popocatapetl and Ixtaccihuatl, or the woman in white, so named for the great resemblance of its summit, which, like that of Popocatapetl, is clothed in eternal snow, to the recumbent form of a woman.

A stroll along the Paseo on a fine afternoon will enable one to form some idea of the wealth and beauty of Mexican society. The fashionable equip-ages—barouches, landaus, broughams, and victorias—drawn by horses of English or American breed, with coachmen and footmen in correct European livery, even to the cockades, or in the picturesque Mexican dress, and occupied by dark-eyed beauties; the buggies and fast-trotters, which have of late become somewhat fashionable; an occasional dog-cart in the thorough English style, or a handsome drag, tooled along by a young Mexican blood who has learnt to handle the ribbons during his university education in England—these are all to be seen, with a good sprinkling of humbler conveyances, from the neat blue-flag victoria to the hearse-like white-flag coach, laden with men, women and children, and drawn by attenuated mules, more fit for the slaughter-house than the garish Paseo de la Reforma.

The paths are filled with a motley crowd of well-dressed people and ragged Indians, among whom the ice-seller is driving a roaring trade. Groups of dudes stand at the edge of the roadway, criticising the fair occupants of the carriages, and seeking to arrest the attention of bewitching eyes by just the same tactics as those adopted by the fraternity in old Rotten Row.

Outside the café are seated groups of different nationalities, as evidenced by the snatches of conversations one overhears in the various European languages, enjoying their refrescos [1] under the shade of the great trees, listening to the strains of the band and watching the varied scene, while obsequious waiters run hither and thither supplying their wants, or carrying ices to the ladies in the carriages at the roadside.

In the far distance stand the blue mountains, sharply defined against the clear sky, whose pale, many-coloured tints are imparted by the rays of the setting sun; and, as the twilight fades, the carriage lights flit about like wills o' the wisp in the gathering darkness, which betokens that the pleasant afternoon on the Paseo is at an end.

On Sunday mornings the fashionable promenade is the Alameda, beginning at 11 A.M. and lasting till 1 P.M. At the time of our arrival the resort of the

[1] Cooling drinks.

élite was the Plaza, or Zocalo as it is called, the
Alameda being then a wilderness, which it was considered unsafe to cross after dusk. The latter has now
been made quite a pretty little park. Well-kept lawns,
laid out in beds of tasteful pattern and resplendent
with flowers of every colour, shaded by the fine old
trees, and edged with geraniums, have taken the place
of the stubbly grass, on which groups of Indians with
their dogs used to be seen taking their *al fresco* meals,
or enjoying their mid-day nap. Handsome fountains
meet the eye wherever the broad paths intersect ;
the quaint Moorish kiosco, formerly occupied by the
Mexican exhibit at New Orleans Exhibition, looks
very picturesque among the trees ; and the regimental
bands discourse sweet music from the pretty music-
stands. The ladies are gay in dresses of all colours,
from delicate cream to flaming scarlet, occasionally
offering contrasts that are not always pleasing; while
the men wear the high hat and patent-leather boots,
so little adapted to a hot, sunny morning, clothes of
pattern and colour sometimes fearful and wonderful
to behold, and carry walking-sticks with handles of
prodigious size.

On the whole, however, it is a well-dressed crowd.
Stately matrons of portly mien escorting their bevies
of dark-eyed daughters, brides leaning confidingly on
their husbands' arms, exquisitely-dressed children
marching solemnly by their parents' side, grey-haired
men whose erect bearing shows their military calling,

dudes assuming the Piccadilly lounge, fair-haired Teutons of heavy build, keen-visaged Americans, self-possessed Englishmen—what an interesting sight they present as they saunter up and down between the lines of chairs, whose occupants are, doubtless, keenly criticising them, or past the group of lagartijos,[1] who lose no opportunity to 'echar flores'[2] to the girls as they pass.

Very different scenes have been enacted on this spot in the days of cruel fanaticism, when the *auto de fé* of the Inquisition was held here, and processions of martyrs were led to the stake for their unwavering adherence to their faith.

The Zocalo, the principal square of the city, bears a fine appearance. The north side is occupied by the cathedral, standing behind pretty gardens full of tea and other beautiful varieties of roses and semi-tropical trees and shrubs, with here and there little mounds covered by different species of cactus and curious Aztec idols. On the east side stands the Palace, while in the west and the south are picturesque old houses built over portales. These portales are the busiest thoroughfares of Mexico; here are all the hat-shops, and most of the cheaper class of dry-goods stores; at each pillar is a little stand, at which toys, newspapers, or cigarettes are sold, and the pavement is crowded with all classes of people in search of bargains.

[1] Lizards, a nickname for loungers.
[2] Literally, throwing flowers—*i.e.* paying compliments in an audible voice.

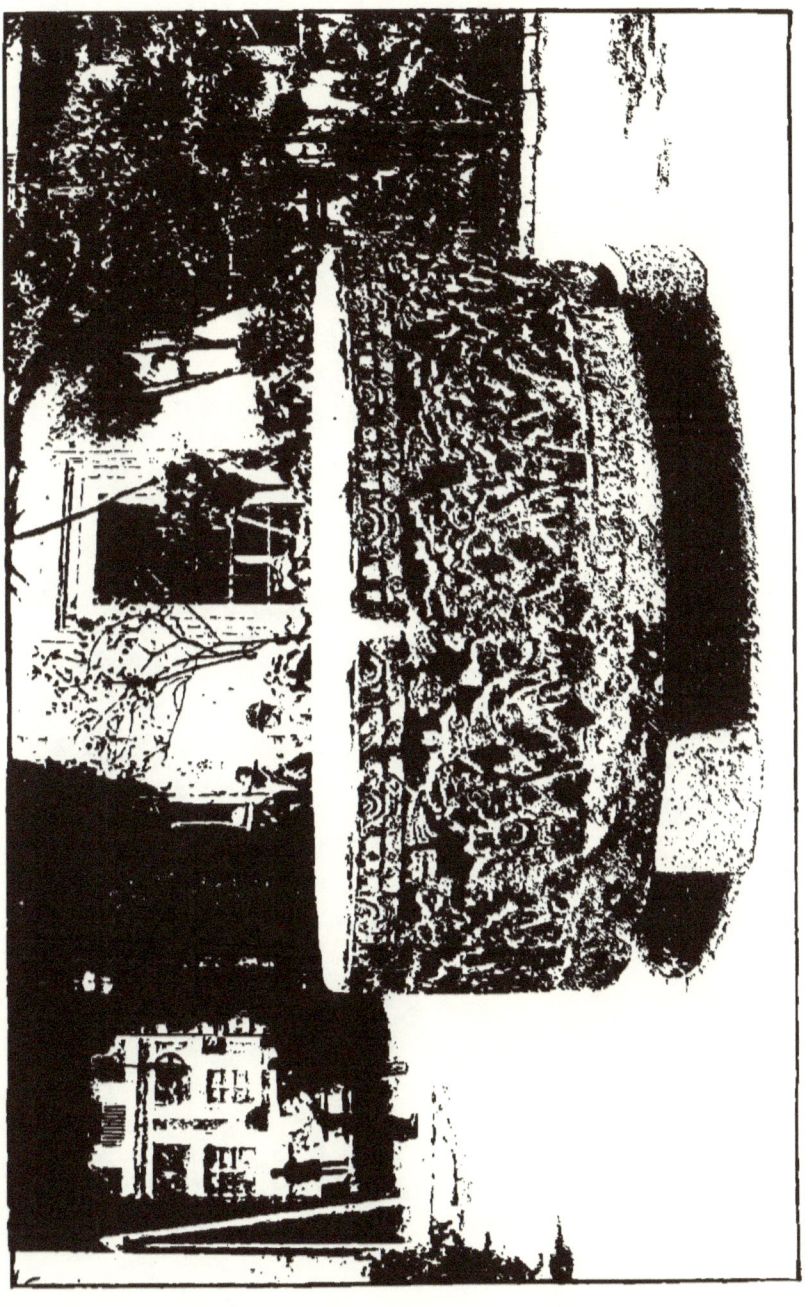

SACRIFICIAL STONE, MEXICO CITY

This is the site of the old square, in the midst of which, according to tradition, stood the Teocalli, or temple of human sacrifice, and around which, probably in arcades similar to the present portales, were the stalls of the cunning workers in gold and silver, and other vendors of the articles of luxury of the day. It was under the Zocalo that the calendar-stone was found—one of Mexico's most highly prized antiquities, covered with hieroglyphics, by which the Aztecs of old knew the seasons of the year and the days of the month. This huge stone, weighing many tons, embedded in the wall of the cathedral until quite recently, has now been transferred to the museum, where it shares with the sacrificial stone the chief attention of visitors to that interesting building.

At the side of the cathedral, and almost opposite Cinco de Mayo Street, is the flower market. On those saints' days which represent the Christian names of most of the Mexican ladies there is a great demand for bouquets; every friend of a lady is expected to present her with a nosegay on her 'dia de santo,'[1] and servants may be seen in all directions bearing these floral offerings with the giver's card stuck in the centre. On these occasions the lady whose saint's day is commemorated has quite a festival of flowers, which fill her corridors, rooms, and even balconies.

Leading from the Zocalo are the principal streets.

[1] Saint's day.

The Plateros, which further on becomes San Francisco Street, may be termed the Broadway of Mexico, for here are all the finest shops and most of the principal hotels. Refugio Street is also full of shops, but of less pretensions. Monterilla is the principal dry-goods street, and Cinco de Mayo, a new street, is the broadest and handsomest of all, but, much to the detriment of trade, blocked at one end by the National Theatre.

The Plateros is the favourite morning rendezvous of the Mexican lagartijos, whose principal resort was ' Micolo's,' the fashionable barber's shop, which has now been closed. In those days all the scandal of the town, all the rumours of revolution and other canards, could be traced to Micolo's. The dudes now assemble at different points on the shady side of the street, their favourite pastime being to ' echar flores ' to the girls. As their compliments are sometimes couched in the broadest terms, many ladies strongly object to being annoyed in this manner, and there are frequent complaints. An American girl effectually put a stop to the annoyance to which she was subjected by these young sparks, one of whom received from her a left-hander, delivered in the most scientific style, which left him all but insensible. It turned out that she was the female athlete of Orrin's circus. After that day the dudes allowed her to pass in the most respectful silence.

Another young American lady, a tourist, struck

one of these young cads full in the face with her sun-shade. Consequently the lagartijos appear to have come to the conclusion that the most prudent course is to confine their attention to the Mexican ladies, and to treat with chilling indifference those of other nationalities, as incapable of appreciating a compliment.

It is a pity that Cinco de Mayo Street, which is composed of fine modern buildings, should be entirely spoiled by being blocked by the National Theatre. Its original intention was to carry it to the Alameda, running from the Zocalo parallel with Plateros and San Francisco Streets, but as the value of property in the centre of the city is so great, the idea had to be abandoned. As it is, the street leads nowhere, and, as hardly any traffic passes through it, the shops which are opened on it are soon closed in preference for busier thoroughfares.

Refugio is an old-fashioned street, full of shops, one of its sides being covered in by portales, under which sit vendors of old books and a medley of odds and ends, which are exposed for sale on the pavement. Their stocks consist of a queer collection of all sorts of old articles—razors, looking-glasses, broken fans, inkstands, spurs, mathematical instruments, carpenters' tools, odd pieces of crockery, surgical instruments, nails and screws, opera-glasses, knives and forks, images of saints, broken decanters, chromos;

in fact, anything and everything that the pelado [1] has been able to pilfer and dispose of for a few cents to these *al fresco* bazaars. On Sunday mornings old copper paintings, Spanish fans, &c., can be picked up here sometimes for a trifle.

The banks and principal houses of commerce are situated in Don Juan Manuel, Cadenas, Capuchinas, San Agustin, and other quiet streets, lying a couple of blocks to the south of San Francisco Street.

[1] Literally, 'close-cropped,' a term used for sneak thieves and others who gain their livelihood by questionable means.

CHAPTER IV

MEXICO is lamentably deficient in hotels. The best, the Iturbide, San Carlos, Guardiola, and Jardin, offer little comfort to the traveller. Only in the Jardin, which is the newest and most attractive, facing a beautiful garden, is there a restaurant upstairs. The Iturbide and San Carlos have a restaurant downstairs, which is under separate management. Little attention is paid to the comfort of the guests, whose best plan, here as elsewhere, is to keep in the good graces of the mozo,[1] by feeing occasionally, but not too largely. The furniture is old and dingy, the carpets threadbare and stained, and the beds leave much to be desired in the matter of softness. These hotels are all clean; that much must be said in their favour; and by slow degrees improvements are being made.

A great change will come soon, for already four concessions have been granted for the erection of

[1] Man-servant.

hotels on a large scale, after the American pattern ; and, no doubt, ere two or three years have passed one or more of these will be completed, and will take away the custom from the old uncomfortable houses with which the traveller has at present to content himself.

Even with the poor accommodation that the city offers to-day, tourists flock to it in crowds, and excur- sions of seventy and eighty at a time constantly arrive between January and June, during which months it is often a matter of difficulty to obtain a room anywhere. The enterprising spirits that will confer a boon on travellers by establishing a first-rate hotel will find it a most lucrative undertaking ; but at first they will have difficulties to contend with in obtaining good attendants and a varied supply of food.

At the restaurants the attendance is bad, the tables very small, and the seats uncomfortable, yet, as in the case of the hotels, it is ' Take it or leave it ! ' Therefore complaints are useless, and all that can be done is to hope for better times. Foreigners will fre- quent one restaurant for a month, then quit it for another, and so on until they return to the first, which they had vowed never to re-enter, and where no surprise is evinced at their return. I have experienced this myself, and know others who have been successively going the round of the restaurants in quest of a good meal all their lives.

The cost of living in Mexico is very high. Rent is perhaps the worst item of all ; it is true that rooms can be rented at hotels for 25 to 30 dollars per month, but house-rent is exorbitant. A decent flat of six or seven rooms cannot be had for less than 40 dollars, and the houses are nearly all large, consisting of ten or twelve rooms at least, the rental ranging from 100 dollars and upwards per month. The system of ' viviendas ' or flats is becoming general, and as fast as houses of this kind are run up the flats are let before they are finished. Their principal drawback is the ' portero ' or ' concierge,' who recognises no master but the landlord, and is a tyrant to the unfortunate tenants. Porteros are generally cobblers by trade. Now, without wishing to hurt the feelings of an industrious class of artisans, I have always heard that the cobbler is, by nature of his calling, narrow-minded and misanthropical. At any rate this is true in Mexico ; your cobbler portero is a misanthrope of the highest order. The only exception that I know of is the portero of the Anglo-American Club, who is always civil and obliging ; but his is an easy and lucrative post, for, besides being well paid, he makes boots for many of the members, and every year he receives a handsome Christmas-box. Those of private houses are often of a superior class, being in many instances superannuated servants of the family. But the portero of a flat-house is a perfect Cerberus ; he has rarely a civil word for the tenants, and takes good care to be well paid for any odd jobs he may do for them. The landlords rarely allow their tenants latch-keys, and, when they do, the keys are of such di-mensions that one almost requires a mozo to carry them.

The portero expects a tip from everyone coming in after 10 p.m., and even then exercises his discretion as to whether they shall be admitted. If he lets the tenant in, it is not before he has driven the unfortu-nate man to the verge of lunacy. Returning from a dance, I remembered to my dismay that I had left the latchkey on our dressing-table ; there was nothing for it but to knock the portero up. Now our par-ticular old gentleman, although his sense of hearing was very acute during the day, once in bed became as deaf as an adder. After wearing out my knuckles on the door ineffectually, my eye fell on a cobble lying in the road. Armed with this, I hammered until the tenants upstairs implored me to stop. My only reply was to redouble my efforts, and finally the old man awoke and let us in. Then, in the darkness of the night, I pummelled him well with the stone, till he prayed for mercy and vowed he would never keep me waiting again.

To return to the cost of living. Female servants' wages are about 10 dollars per month, mozos earn 20 dollars to 25 dollars, and coachmen 30 dollars to 35 dollars monthly. Meat, vegetables, eggs, and milk are, generally speaking, about the same price as in London. The soul of the tenant, though not vexed with water, gas, and poor-rates, is burdened by indirect taxation. Owing to the high tariff, imported goods are very dear.

In considering the cost of living it should be borne in mind that it is compensated for by the considerable profits made by the merchants, and the high salaries of employés as compared with other countries. Those occupying responsible positions often receive very high salaries. There is little demand for clerks in Mexico; most of the foreign houses bring out their employés under contract, and it would be unwise for anyone without some little capital to go out in search of employment. But he must not hope to find an 'El Dorado.' He will have to work harder than in England; but, with steadiness and industry, he will have ample opportunities of getting on. Those who have a capital of from 2,000*l.* upwards can do better with their money here than elsewhere, provided they have some knowledge of the language, and proper caution be used. There are many ways of making money in Mexico, and, as the country becomes more developed these will increase. Commerce, cattle-raising, timber-cutting, tobacco, sugar and coffee growing, and mining, all hold out great inducements, and the amount of English capital invested in cattle ranches and mining enterprises, though large, is a trifle compared to the openings that occur daily for the advantageous investment of money.

The country is so large, and the districts being opened up by the railroads are so fertile and rich in minerals, that there is ample room for the employment of many times the amount already invested by foreign capitalists in Mexico.

The commerce of Mexico City is very considerable, as it has always been the distributing point for the whole country, from its proximity to Vera Cruz. The effect of the railroads must, however, be felt eventually by the diversion of some of its trade. Although its commercial supremacy will not be seriously threatened, owing to its being the seat of Government, San Luis Potosi bids fair to be a rival in course of time, from its central position and railroad communication with Tampico. All the leading houses in the capital are Spanish, French, German, and English, in their order of precedence as given here. The Spaniards devote themselves mostly to the grocery business. The French come next in number, and confine themselves almost entirely to dry-goods, fancy articles, tailoring, and dressmaking; while the Germans, who also do some banking, are the owners of the hardware stores. The English colony is a small one, comprising the managers of important London companies and their subordinates, and a few others connected with railroad and mining enterprises. The Americans are chiefly engaged in mining and railroads. Owing to the limited number of the purchasing classes, the necessities of the Indians being confined to cheap cloth and hardware, Mexico is essentially a low-priced market. Cheap showy goods—German imitations of English cutlery, &c.—find most favour; and it is only articles of luxury, which the rich affect, that fetch high prices. The Mexican is a shrewd buyer, and a conservative in his tastes; he will never buy any article without carefully examining it, and takes care not to pay a cent more than he can help. He always prefers a make that he knows, and requires considerable persuasion to be induced to try a new mark or brand.

Throughout the country the shops are named according to the caprice of the owners, whose names seldom appear outside. The names given are generally appropriate to the branch of business. A shoemaker's shop will be styled 'El pié del Sílfide' (the Sylph's foot); a hat shop 'El sombrero rojo' (the red hat), and so on; whilst in others the appropriateness of the name is not considered. A grocer's store is named 'El Borrego' (the sheep); a little tobacco-shop will aspire to the title of 'El Universo' (the universe); a pulqueria, 'El Venus Negro' (the black Venus); and there is a bar-room in one of the worst parts of the city, in which rows are of constant occurrence, that seeks to hide its vice under the name of 'Los Capuchinos' (the Capuchins).

Commercial credit is good, failures being rare,

and the Americans are making great efforts to introduce their manufactures; but until they study the
language of the country and the needs of the market,
pay greater attention to the packing of goods and
the execution of orders, and are willing to offer the
long credits given by European merchants, they will
not make much progress.

The shopkeepers have no lack of enterprise, as
is shown by their eagerness to obtain all the latest
fashions and novelties, and the money they spend in
advertising—newspapers, walls, and tramcars being
full of advertisements. Even the drop-curtain of the
theatres is let out for this purpose, so that the audience may have ample opportunity of learning between
the acts which is the best saloon, the cheapest steamship line, or most effective cure for corns, from the
fantastic paintings before them.

The principal daily newspapers are the 'Monitor
Republicano,' 'El Tiempo,' 'Siglo XIX.,' 'Universal,'
and 'Diario del Hogar,' while the 'Two Republics'
and the 'Anglo-American' are the organs of the
English and Americans, the 'Trait d'Union' of the
French, and the 'Diario Español' of the Spanish.
The 'Mexican Financier,' published weekly in English
and Spanish, is an excellent paper. Its reading
matter consists generally of topics of commercial
interest, thoughtfully discussed, and its articles are
above suspicion of pandering to the Government.
The 'Monitor Republicano' is of thorough inde-

pendent tenets. In fact, it is so independent that, in perusing its articles, one is tempted to wonder whether anything could satisfy it. It is always full of criticisms on the Government and on Mexicans generally, but especially on the conduct of the 'Yankees,' or 'Ayankados,' as I have seen it written on the railroads, &c. It is laughable to see how the 'Monitor' introduces English words, occasionally slightly altering them. One reads a paragraph gravely stating that 'the highlifistas' of Mexico will have a gay season, or that two 'gentlemen' had a difference in San Francisco Street, which resulted in the one who was most proficient in ' the box ' knocking the other down. In its Sunday issue the 'Monitor' has always a set of articles devoted to the topics of the week, ladies' fashions, &c. The gentleman who, under the *nom de plume* 'Juvenal,' delights the Mexicans with his sprightly witticisms in these articles, got into trouble one day and nearly lost his life. It appears that in a previous Sunday's issue he had referred to a new style of hat that he had noticed, in his usual manner, and a lady who had worn a similar hat took the criticism as meant for her head-dress. The cap fitted with a vengeance. She called upon him for an explanation. Finding that her repeated visits were growing troublesome, he gave orders that in future he was 'not at home' to her. The enraged woman met him one day as he was entering the Iturbide Hotel, and fired at him with a revolver, wounding him in the hand before the astonished spectators were able to wrest the weapon from her.

The newspaper offices close at 5 P.M. By that time the following morning's paper has been prepared ; by 9 P.M. it is printed and the paper-boys are shouting in the streets, ' To-morrow's paper ! ' The editor of a newspaper must exert great discretion, for not only is the fear of the libel law before his eye, but any disrespectful criticism of the powers that be will result in his making unwilling acquaintance with the interior of the Belem jail, ' preso é incomunicado.' [1] As Belem is crowded with prisoners of the worst stamp, amongst whom typhoid fever and small-pox are often prevalent, and its cells are not of the cleanest or most commodious description, it follows that editors have a natural aversion to it, especially as, once in, it is quite an open question when the delinquent will get out again. President Diaz, on his accession, found the Press far too outspoken, and promptly silenced some of the editors by sending them to Belem. At one time there was quite a number imprisoned, and the clamour raised by the papers failed to liberate them. When, after having been kept in durance vile for some considerable time, they were released, the lesson proved effectual, for they have taken good care not to offend again.

[1] ' In solitary confinement.'

This to English ears sounds shocking, but in dealing with these people such measures are often necessary to avoid the risk of revolutions and bloodshed. Comic papers are occasionally started, but as they consist of skits on the Government and private individuals, their proprietors often find their way to Belem. Speaking of comic papers reminds me of a French paper published under the title of ' Le Petit Gaulois,' several years ago, by a keen-witted Frenchman. It was a bright, amusing little paper, in true Parisian style, and its editor, while sharp enough to keep clear of the libel laws, was constantly in hot water in consequence of his trenchant sarcasms, several duels being the result. As he always came off victorious in these encounters, and did not hesitate to chuckle over them in his next week's paper, his adversaries concluded that it was best to submit to his ridicule in silence. But one day he made a mistake, by offering a gratuitous insult to the Queen of England. The attention of the English Minister having been called to this, he at once laid the matter before the President, the result of which was that the editor of ' Le Petit Gaulois ' was punished, and had to insert an apology in his paper. There are numbers of other periodicals in Mexico, and it is perhaps as well supplied in this respect as any city in newer countries, *so far as numbers go*, but I doubt whether their owners make money out of

E

them. I believe the only paper that has made its owner's fortune is the 'Monitor Republicano,' for which $250,000 has been offered by some Americans.

Constant complaints are made by the Press of the high tariff on printing paper, and efforts have been made to obtain a reduction in the import duties, but I do not think that the public would reap much profit thereby. Whatever gain resulted would go to the newspaper proprietors. What is wanted in the daily papers is more enterprise and better telegraphic news ; were proper attention paid to these important points, their circulation would increase proportionately. Now that all the principal American newspapers have their correspondents in the city, the outside world is made acquainted with news from Mexico of which the Mexicans are often ignorant. These correspondents are sometimes not as prudent as they should be, and in their desire to obtain startling news they are not always careful to verify the reports. Hence a good deal of harm has been done to the country by the *canards* published abroad. But this is not so much the case now; foreigners, and especially Americans, have visited the country in such numbers of late that it is much better understood than formerly, and reports which a few years ago would have had credence would be treated with incredulity now. The prompt manner in which false reports have been contradicted by the

Government, and by foreign correspondents of standing, has also done much to bring about a better state of things, and the news now sent from Mexico can be generally relied upon, although there is still room for improvement.

CHAPTER V

Lotteries—The Zoological Lottery—Gambling houses—Bull-fights—
Riot in a bull-ring—A bull-fight procession—Lassoing—A duel
with lassos—Mexican horsemanship—The coleadero—Cock-
fighting—Foreign sports.

ONE of the most important revenues of the Government is derived from the lotteries. At every corner,
in every shop, restaurant, and saloon, are the lottery-
ticket sellers. One hears their cries at every step,
and the manner in which people are constantly im-
portuned to buy such and such a lucky number is
very annoying. I saw a small boy hurrying along
shouting his lottery tickets, and as he passed me he
dropped one. Calling after him, I gave him the
ticket, which I had picked up. He seemed very grateful and thanked me profusely. As I turned to go, he
begged me to buy the ticket, saying that my kindness
would surely bring me luck. Amused at his sharpness,
I bought it, although not a believer in these lotteries,
and afterwards learned that this was a favourite
trick of the lottery-ticket sellers, who, of course,
take good care that a confederate is on the watch to
see that no one decamps with the ticket which has

been dropped. There are not only the Government lotteries; there are also those of the 'Beneficencia Pública,' a company started by a number of Mexicans and Americans, who obtained the concession on condition that a stated proportion of the profits of the concern should be devoted to works of public charity or utility; and the smaller lotteries in favour of hospitals and charitable institutions, both in and out of Mexico, the prizes ranging from 1 to 100,000 dollars. This affords occupation to a host of men, women, and children, who seem to earn quite a little living in this manner. They must have a Government licence, and are, as a rule, fairly honest; but it is suspected that pickpockets make use of this disguise to exercise their calling. An enterprising Frenchman introduced the Zoological Lottery in the early part of 1890; and as the prizes were small, the prices of the tickets ranging from 5 cents to 1 dollar, little attention was paid to it at first. As the scheme was widely advertised, and the low prices of the tickets placed them within the reach of school children, servants, and even the poorest classes, in a short time it attracted the attention of all. Everyone took tickets, from the highest to the lowest, and the Plaza San Juan, where the winning animal for each day's lottery was exhibited at six o'clock, was so completely blocked that the inhabitants could not leave their houses. Every evening a vast crowd collected, comprising all classes; fashionably dressed people jostled with ragged Indians, and many came in their carriages to ascertain their luck. The Press called the attention of the Government to the evil being wrought among the needy classes by a system of lottery which was nothing but a game of faro; and one fine morning it was suspended. The system was simplicity itself. The names of twenty-five animals were selected; and at seven in the morning the manager placed in a box a figure of the animal that was to represent the prize number of the day, and this was exhibited in the Plaza that evening. The winner obtained twenty-four times the sum he had invested, and the profits of the Company were represented as 4 per cent. But they must have been much higher, for I have known the shares jump from 30 to 300 dollars in a week, and had the lottery continued they would have attained a fabulous value.

A newspaper asserted that there was nothing easier than for the manager to select as winning animal one that from the sales of the previous day was evidently not a favourite with the public, and which, therefore, would probably not be in much demand. However this may be, the scheme made a fortune for its projectors during the short time it lasted.

The story runs that on one occasion the manager, as he was putting the winning animal for the day in the box, detected a small boy watching him through the keyhole. Opening the door suddenly, he angrily asked the boy what he had seen. The lad tremblingly confessed that he had seen a serpent put into the box. The manager evinced the greatest annoyance, and made the boy promise that he would not divulge the secret. As the shrewd director had foreseen, there was an enormous demand for serpents that day; the evening came, and at the time appointed the winning animal was exhibited—it was a lion.

A land where the inhabitants are, to a man, born gamblers is an El Dorado for the proprietors of gambling hells; vast fortunes have been made in this manner, the monopoly in Mexico City being held by a ring of wealthy men. These dens are of all descriptions, from the aristocratic houses in Tacubaya, standing in beautiful grounds, and replete with every luxury, where players are supplied with refreshments and conveyed to the city in special cars provided for the purpose, free of charge, to places where those of modest means may gratify their passion for play. Excellent order is maintained in these establishments, disturbances being of rare occurrence. There is a certain house in Refugio Street, to all appearances a private dwelling-place of respectable exterior. Its number is sixteen, and as 'No. 16' it is known to the Mexicans and tourists, who visit it as one of the sights of Mexico. This seems to be a favourite gambling house, and probably does more business than any of its more aristocratic rivals, being filled nightly with crowds intent upon trying their luck.

The passion for play pervades all classes, even foreigners not being exempt from it. Vast sums and valuable estates are won or lost in a night in princely residences in the suburbs, and men who from their position and opportunities should be millionaires are often reduced to very straitened circumstances. To this vice may be attributed in a great measure the dishonesty of the lower orders and the abject poverty of which one sees so much.

Another evil that has a pernicious effect, especially among the lower orders, is the bull-fight. The peon will sell his shirt, and the servant will rob his master, sooner than lose a chance of seeing his favourite bull-fighter kill a bull. Formerly these spectacles were illegal in the city district, and the taurophiles had to go some distance by tramcar or rail to indulge their propensities. But of late years they have been legalised within the city limits, and it is unfortunate that the former law should have been repealed. Hardly had the new edict been promulgated than six bull-rings were hastily constructed, all unsightly wooden structures that had little appearance of safety, two of them being erected, as though in mockery of public opinion, at either corner of the Paseo, completely marring the effect of the entrance. Almost the first question asked by tourists is when and where the next bull-fight is to be held, and the ladies, with rare exceptions, in spite of all dissuasion, seem the most anxious to attend. Some American tourists once questioned me on the subject, and, although I did my utmost to point out to the ladies of the party what a cruel, disgusting spectacle it was, they persisted in their determination to see it. I know one gentleman who boasts that he has never missed a bull-fight since he has been in the country, and has even been carried from a sick bed to witness one. Among the Mexicans they are universally patronised, members of the aristocracy being appointed presidentes, or judges. The position of a judge requires some tact, for here the mob is virtually ruler. The foreigner has no conception of the keen interest with which the movements of the bull-fighters and of the animals are watched and criticised. A cricket-match at Lord's will not receive the absorbing attention with which the Mexican watches his bull-fight, and in a spectacle where several thousands are present, all of whom thoroughly understand the science, the *vox populi* must be respected. If a bull-fighter makes a mistake he is unmercifully hooted, and if he repeats the error, or shows the white feather, he may be pelted with chairs and every plank that can be torn from the seats. On the other hand, a brilliant stroke or a clever feat is rewarded with rapturous applause, cigars, hats, fruit, bonbons, and money are showered into the ring. A bull-ring was nearly demolished one Sunday because the bulls were bad, and by the time the guards had cleared the ring it was almost a ruin.

The 'cuadrilla,' as the body of performers in the ring is called, consists of the 'espada,' who controls the whole; the 'picadores,' or horsemen; the 'capeadores,' who flaunt their red cloaks in the face of the bull, in order to distract his attention from a fallen comrade or get the animal into any required position; and the 'banderilleros,' who fix the darts in the bull's shoulders. There is also the butcher, who gives the *coup de grâce* as the poor beast lies dying, by driving a sharp dagger into his head; and the lassoers, whose duty it is to lasso and drag from the ring a bull which will not fight.

It is a pretty sight to watch the procession as it enters the ring at the commencement of the afternoon's proceedings.

At its head, on a beautiful, highly trained horse, rides the chamberlain, in the dress of the old Spanish style, while his steed paces gracefully, as though proud of the position he occupies; then follow the 'capeadores' and 'banderilleros,' in their handsome open jackets of red, green, yellow, or blue satin, heavy with gold or silver embroidery, disclosing elaborately embroidered shirts, with broad silken sashes round the waist, and knee-breeches to match the jackets, white stockings, and neat-fitting slippers, while a curious three-cornered astrachan cap covers the head, from which hangs behind the short, well-greased pigtail, emblem of their calling, and of which they are as proud as any Chinaman. Next come the 'picadores,' sitting stiffly in their leather suits and stuffed leggings on the scraggy, blindfolded horses. Behind them walks the ' espada,' carrying his short capa and keen, rapier-like sword, while a team of gaily caparisoned mules, held in control with difficulty by running footmen, prance in the rear.

The procession, sallying from the door, marches across the ring to the president's box opposite, where the chamberlain, stopping his horse in a perfect attitude of grace, asks for the keys. These are thrown to him, and dexterously caught in his hat; then, wheeling round, he canters off, and disappears through the gateway, from which the bull issues immediately afterwards. The bull-fighters have, in the meantime, taken up their positions in the ring, which is encircled by a stout barricade about seven feet high, having at intervals refuges formed by a short outer barricade, at a sufficient distance from the inner one to enable the bull-fighters to glide behind them when hard pressed, but not wide enough to admit of the bull's horns passing. The bull-fighters, with the exception of the picador, have thus two means of escape—by vaulting over the barricade, which they do with the greatest ease and agility, or slipping behind the refuge. For the picador there is no chance of escape. Mounted on his emaciated horse, which has been sold for the purpose because his days are numbered, or he has some defect that renders him useless to man, his rider must await the onslaught of the bull, and trust to his firm seat and strength of arm to keep the animal at bay with his long, stout lance.   These men are as perfect as a Hercules, and, as a rule, defend their horses well.   Sitting immovable in their saddles, they bear the full force of the bull's attack on the lance, with which they skillfully ward it off.   This is when the animal charges in front or at the side; but when he delivers the attack from behind, the poor horse, whose trembling limbs have lost their activity, cannot answer quickly enough to rein and spur, and in a moment is lifted in the air, falling heavily to the ground with his rider.   Instantly the capeadores surround the bull, distracting his attention with their capas,[1] while the picador is disentangled from his horse, which he at once remounts, if it can be got to stand by dint of kicks and blows. Then follows a shocking sight; the poor beast staggers along gashed and bleeding, is forced again and again to face the bull, until a final stroke puts an end to its sufferings.

I shall not attempt to describe a bull-fight in detail.   Previous writers have made English readers familiar enough with the brutality and horrors of the arena, as well as with the display of inhumanity and of low, animal instincts amongst the audience. Happy the day, both for Spain and Mexico, when such spectacles no longer receive the sanction of law and the approval of the people.

---

[1] A cloak of red cloth.

Lassoing is another favourite diversion. Riding at full gallop, the horseman pursues the bull in its headlong flight; in an instant the lasso flashes in a curve through the air, alighting on the feet or horns, the noose is drawn tight, the horse stops dead, the lasso, wound round the peak of the saddle, strains as though it would break, and the bull falls with a heavy thud. The instinct of the horses is wonderful. They are trained to stop the moment the lasso tightens, and, throwing their bodies into an attitude which enables them to withstand the shock, they keep a steady pull on the bull so that he cannot move.

While I was in Mexico a duel with lassoes occurred. Two vaqueros [1] agreed to settle their differences in this manner. Out on the plains they met, and for a long time dodged each other's lassoes, until at last the fatal noose fell over the neck of one. His horse, true to its instinct, stopped short on feeling a strain on the saddle, and its rider was jerked instantly from his saddle with a broken neck, the victor dragging the lifeless body at full gallop several miles.

It is hardly necessary to say that Mexicans excel in horsemanship. As boys they learn to ride as soon as they can walk, and it is no uncommon thing to see a lad of five or six years of age managing with perfect ease a full-grown horse. The rein is a slight cord of horsehair, held in the forefinger, the bit being so severe that the horse answers to the slightest touch.

[1] Cowboys.

Many of these animals are very spirited, and nothing delights a Mexican so much as showing off his equestrian skill. The saddles are heavy, but do not gall the animal's back, and are very comfortable for long journeys, especially when, as is generally the case, mountains have to be climbed. They are made of hard wood covered with parchment drawn tight, and have a peak for lassoing, a narrow open space running along the middle. A thick blanket protects the horse's back from the frame of the saddle. The spurs used are enormous, weighing as much as eight or ten pounds the pair, but are not so cruel as they look, for the rowels, which are two or three inches in diameter, are blunt, and do not inflict as much punishment as our small English spurs. Ladies, in riding, rest the leg over the peak—a position which appears to be very comfortable, and quite as graceful as when an English saddle is used.

'Colear'[1] is also a favourite pastime, and requires considerable skill and knack. The horseman gallops close by the side of the bull, on a level with its hindquarters, and, catching the tail firmly in his hand, adroitly twists it round the animal's foot, and turns it over on its side. The young bloods are very fond of this, and occasionally a 'coleadero,' as a spectacle of this kind is called, is given to some distinguished personage or foreigner to whom they wish to show attention.

[1] To catch by the tail.

The passion for cock-fighting appears to prevail mostly in the interior. A long, curved, keen blade is attached to the bird's leg in the place of the natural spur, and the combat is only of a moment's duration, at the end of which the defeated bird lies transfixed by one quick stab to the heart. Wherever one goes are gamecocks, some of excellent breed, as much as fifty dollars being asked for the best, the average price varying from five to ten dollars. So far as I have been able to observe, the only pleasure derived from this sport is in the opportunity afforded for gambling, and I have known as much as 1,000 dollars a side laid on a single combat. I do not think there is any cock-pit in the city, nor do I remember ever having seen the advertisement of a cock-fight, unless for the suburbs, or a fair in some town in the interior.

Of late polo and lawn-tennis have found a good many votaries among the Mexican aristocracy and some members of the English and other foreign colonies. A polo club has been in existence for some time, and some gentlemen keep capital polo ponies. A boating club is also being got up among the English and Americans, which several Mexicans have already joined.

CHAPTER VI

Mexican and foreign clubs—Theatres—The 'Mayer' incident—
Patti's reception—Orrin's circus—Cafés—The 5th of May—
The 16th of September—The Rurales—Cuauhtemoc anniversary
—The Combate de Flores—Feast days on the Viga—The
Chinampas.

THERE are a number of clubs in the city, the Jockey
Club being the most aristocratic and select. It was
organised by a number of Mexican gentlemen with
a view to the encouragement of horse-racing and
providing a social club. Each contributed 1,000
dollars towards its foundation and the purchase
of a race-course. The founders have the greater
part of the control, and it is the best-managed and
most flourishing institution of its kind. It has succeeded in its object of popularising horse-racing, and
has by this means been the cause of much improvement in the breed of horses. Some of those competing have been brought from England, and are
as good as many to be seen on a European course.
Race meetings are very popular ; the course is kept in
good condition, and there is a fine grand-stand, which
is crowded at every meeting by ladies in fashionable
toilettes.

The Albion Club was founded by a number of Englishmen in 1882. To give it wider scope the Americans were invited to join it, and its name was altered to the Anglo-American Club. It is a pleasant sociable club, and in its comfortable rooms the prominent members of both colonies may usually be met in the evenings after the day's business is over. The German Club is universally popular. The Germans form a larger and more wealthy community than the English and Americans, and the large German houses contribute liberally towards the support of an institution which offers suitable recreation to their employés.

The Spaniards have a handsome club-house in a fine old mansion at the corner of Coliseo and San Francisco Streets, which has recently been redecorated and refurnished in a costly manner.

The French have the Philharmonique, which name has been changed to the Cercle Français, and an entrance-fee is now charged. This has no doubt been decided upon to make it more select, and to meet the expenses of the fine new rooms in which the club has recently been installed.

The city of Mexico is very deficient in good theatres. It is strange that a city, whose inhabitants can pay such high prices to attend representations in which Sarah Bernhardt and other notable artistes appear, and concerts at which Adelina Patti, Scalchi, and far-famed tenors sing, cannot

F

afford a handsome theatre. Mexico's two principal theatres, although large buildings, are unworthy of a cultured city. Still, they are crammed from floor to ceiling when any good company is performing, and I should imagine that no impresario who understands his business can have reason to complain of his profits.

Speaking of theatres reminds me of the incident that occurred before the arrival of Patti on her first visit. An individual arrived in Mexico, putting up at the Iturbide Hotel, where he secured handsome rooms, and, giving his name as Mayer, announced that he had arrived to make the necessary preparations for Patti's arrival. As it was well known that Patti's agent was named Mayer, this caused no remark, and he proceeded to lease the theatre for a term of nights, having persuaded an American resident to become security for the rent. He then advertised in the papers that the next day the box-office would be open, when boxes and seats could be secured for the performance, which was to consist of four nights, the various programmes of which he published.

A number of Mexican speculators had been watching for the advent of Patti's agent, and the following morning the crowd of well-dressed people at the theatre doors was so great that police were required to maintain order. Many had been waiting since six in the morning in hopes of being first; and the greatest excitement prevailed.

Before the office closed for the day all the boxes and best places had been secured by the speculators; and I heard of one man who bought up the whole of the gallery. The affair coming to the Governor's ears, he determined upon investigating the matter. Accordingly that evening a police officer waited upon Mayer and informed him that, for the greater security of the public, such a large sum as he had received should be placed in safe keeping. Mayer promptly replied that he should be happy to comply with the Governor's request, which was most reasonable, and suggested that, as the banks were closed at that hour, the money should be deposited with the hotel manager, to be kept in his safe at the disposal of the Governor. The officer agreed to this proposal, and accompanied him to the office, when Mayer, taking a large roll of bank-notes from his pocket, asked the manager for an envelope, in which he enclosed them. He sealed the packet, remarking that as it contained a large sum of money, nearly 40,000 dollars, he hoped that very great precaution would be taken for its safety. The money was locked up in the safe; the officer left; and shortly afterwards Mayer went out. Next evening it was found that he had not slept at the hotel, and on opening the envelope it was discovered that the contents amounted to 400 dollars in bills of small denominations. The alarm was given, and telegraphic instructions were sent to all the railroad stations in

the country to stop and arrest the man. But he was
never caught. It was ascertained that after quitting
the hotel he went to the office of the Central Railroad and asked for a special engine, in order to catch
the night mail, which had started an hour before,
stating that he had received a telegram from Patti
advising him that she would shortly arrive at El
Paso, the frontier station, and therefore it was
absolutely necessary that he should be there to meet
her. An engine was at once provided, for which he
paid 100 dollars. Although the conductor of the train
stated that he had boarded it, all traces of him
were lost, and how he left the country was never
ascertained. It is believed that he got away with
30,000 dollars belonging to a few rich men, who lost
their money in their anxiety to speculate with the
public by purchasing the seats and reselling at a
heavy profit.

When Patti heard of it she decided to give more
representations than had originally been determined
upon, in order to make some amends to the Mexican
public for the cruel hoax. Speculators were again at
work when the real Mayer arrived, and they secured
all the best places; but they were again bitten, for the
public refused to be victimised, and would not pay
more than the legitimate prices, and in some cases
even less. The end of the fictitious Mayer was
tragic. He was arrested afterwards in New York
for forgery, and held to answer other charges from

Europ e,for he proved to be the Benson who was
wanted for having embezzled a considerable sum
from a French marchioness, by means of a betting
office that he had opened in England some years
before. As he feared that the Mexican Government
would demand and obtain his extradition, his horror
of a Mexican jail was so great that he committed
suicide.

Patti was received with the greatest cordiality.
Many gentlemen went on horseback to meet her at the
station and escorted her to the hotel, where violets were
showered upon her, and during her stay she was
much fêted. The President gave a banquet in her
honour at Chapultepec; his wife made her a most
handsome present; and everything that was possible
was done to enable her to carry away pleasant recollections of her visit.

Orrin's circus, which belongs to two brothers,
Americans, is a favourite place of amusement with
both Mexicans and foreigners. The performances are
excellent, and the full houses with which the proprietors are rewarded show that their endeavours to
meet the approval of the public are properly appre-
ciated.

There are two cafés in the city, the Concordia
and the Colon, in the Paseo. The success of the
latter, which is the first open-air café ever opened in
Mexico, should encourage the establishment of others.
One would think that the pleasant outdoor café life,

for which the climate is so admirably adapted, would be more general in Mexico than it is.

The national festivals fall on May 5 and September 16, when all business is suspended and the nation rejoices throughout the country. May 5 is the anniversary of the victory over the French in 1862, and September 16 is that of the Declaration of Independence by the patriot Hidalgo. The military processions are well worth seeing, for it is on such occasions that the stranger can form an opinion of Mexico's army, as the regiments of the different branches defile through the streets of the city.

The finest set of men are the Rurales, or Rural Guards. This corps was founded by President Diaz as a mounted police, and is a most useful body of men. Evil tongues hint that many have distinguished themselves in the days of revolutions and general insecurity as noted brigands. At any rate, they have proved a great success in tracking criminals, and ridding the country of highway robbers, who had inspired terror by their boldness, and whose strongholds in the most inaccessible parts of the mountains can only be discovered by the Rurales. Thanks to the energetic measures of the President, aided by these brave men, the country has been cleared of highwaymen, and is perfectly safe to travel in throughout the interior. In all my travels I have never been molested, my only apprehensions being caused by fellow-passengers in diligencias, who persisted in discussing the relative merits and mechanism of their revolvers, to the imminent danger of a sudden jolt causing the discharge of the weapons.

The uniform of the Rurales is very picturesque and serviceable. It consists of buckskin jacket and trousers embroidered with narrow white braid, and grey felt hats bearing the number of the regiment in silver. The men are armed with carbines, sabres, and revolvers. They are all picked men of great strength and daring, and are mounted on strong serviceable animals, which are kept in good condition. Altogether their appearance is very creditable, and, from the expression of their faces, the evildoer may expect little mercy at their hands.

The Cavalry are also good. The Seventh, commanded by General Gonzales—who, I believe, is not related to the former President of that name—a handsome man of distinguished air, who takes a great pride in his corps, is the crack regiment.

On these festival days processions of the different industrial societies form a prominent part of the proceedings, defiling through the streets for hours, followed by all the rag-tag and bob-tail of the city. San Francisco Street is adorned with huge arches profusely decorated with flowers, and banners floating from poles erected at intervals.

Another interesting ceremony is that recently inaugurated to commemorate the anniversary of the torture inflicted by Cortes on Cuauhtemoc, the Aztec

emperor. On this occasion the President, accompanied
by a numerous cortège, proceeds to the Cuauhtemoc
monument, and, from a pavilion erected to represent
the Aztec style of architecture, listens to the speeches
of Mexican orators, and witnesses the dances of the
Indians, who, dressed in the feather head-dress and
curious garb of the Aztec period, perform mysterious and quaint evolutions with great solemnity,
accompanied by weird, melancholy chants.

I was present at the first 'Combate de Flores,'[1]
which was held in 1890. The idea was originated by
a Frenchman, and having met with the approval of
the aristocracy and the foreign colonies, no expense
was spared to make it a success. But the fun and
frolic which gives such zest to its enjoyment in
Europe were singularly tame. Mexicans, like the
Englishmen, take their pleasures sadly. The flower-
throwing, the laughter, the buffoonery, all seemed too
stiff and formal to be evoked by a genuine mirthful
spirit.

One of the most popular resorts on feast days is
the Viga Canal, on which scores of canoes may be
seen wending their way to Sta. Anita or Ixtacalco,
little villages where picnics and dances are the order
of the day.

Further on are the 'Chinampas,' or floating
gardens, the market gardens of the capital, from
which the Indians in their canoes carry their

[1] Flower combat.

fragrant cargoes of vegetables and flowers to the city. These floating gardens are little islands, divided by narrow strips of water just wide enough to admit a canoe, and with their primitive huts, surrounded by sweet peas, poppies, roses, onions, cabbages, &c., in wild confusion, are very picturesque. Originally these 'Chinampas' were formed by a quantity of weeds, upon which little by little, whether by the hand of man or nature is not known, earth accumulated, forming a fertile soil on which flowers and grass sprung up. These layers, having increased by slow degrees, are to-day several feet in thickness, and the islands thus formed are kept in position by the weeds growing below, which have intertwined themselves around the bottom and sides. Here, even on the Viga, are the signs of ever encroaching civilisation : a concession has been granted to run small naphtha steam-launches, and the quaint old dug-outs, propelled by the swarthy, half-naked Indians, will perhaps some day be a thing of the past.

CHAPTER VII

Courtship in Mexico—Mexican society—Mexican gestures—The hand-shake—Polite expressions — 'Señoras'—Mexican dress—Foreigners in Mexican dress—National drinks.

PERHAPS nothing shows the patience of the Mexican character more than their method of courtship. In Mexico it is the *patient* heart that wins the fair lady. An impatient adorer never achieved the conquest. When a young gentleman takes a fancy to a lady, he follows her to her house, at a respectful distance, and then begins to 'hacer el oso.'[1] Day after day he takes up the same position in a convenient doorway opposite her house, where he will wait for hours to catch a glimpse of the face, or even the hand, of the fair object of his adoration, who is, no doubt, watching for an opportunity to appear at the window.

When at length 'Juliet' steps on to her balcony, a conversation is carried on by signs, and even whispers, which are all clearly caught by the interested parties, though inaudible to passers-by; they seem to understand each other by the motion of the

[1] Literally, ' do the bear.'

lips. I have often wondered at the mysterious structure of the Mexican lover's neck, which enables him to crane it forward during the long conversation carried on with the lady at the window above. I have known one faithful lover standing at his post, always in the same attitude and at the same hour, for four years! When, one day, he disappeared from his post, I ascertained that he had been 'allowed to call' on the young lady for whom he had so long and so patiently waited and watched. No doubt his faithful watch has been by this time rewarded by the hand of his sweetheart.

But when the stern parents have given him permission to call, a lover is never allowed an interview alone with the object of his affection ; a member of the family or a duenna is always present. A Mexican love-suit then becomes expensive, for the lady costs him much more than the average American girl, whose consumption of ice-creams strikes terror into the heart of her impecunious lover. Does he wish to take his beloved one to the theatre, or entertain her at a restaurant ? The whole family will accompany them at his expense; and a Mexican family is numerous as a rule.

At marriage the bridegroom provides the whole trousseau. Once married, his wife takes him in hand, and his purse too. Henceforth, if he wants money he must get it from his better half.

The life of a Mexican married woman must be

very monotonous. Although no expense is grudged for the education of the sons, the women are rarely highly educated, and her only resource is her children and household matters. There is no society, in our sense of the word; families rarely visit each other, and are divided into small cliques.

Parents are devotedly attached to their children. It is pretty to see the little ones kiss the hands of their father as they enter a room, and, in the interior, children, before they can talk, are educated to stand before the visitor with their arms crossed in an attitude of submission, which is meant to convey the words, 'I kiss your hands.' This expression is inherited from Spain, but is not used in Mexico, as in that country, among grown-up people; nor is the polite expression, 'A los pies de usted' ('I am at your feet'), with which a gentleman bows himself from the presence of a Spanish lady, at all current in Mexico. One often sees grown-up sons kiss the hand of their father in the streets, and the Indian always salutes his priest in this manner.

The Mexican is never happy away from his home and relations; this feeling is strong through all classes. No matter how kindly a servant may be treated, if he is from another town he is always pining to return to his relatives, and will leave his situation at any moment for that purpose.

The Mexican gestures are peculiar to this people. Ladies, saluting friends at a distance, make a graceful little gesture of recognition by holding the right-hand palm upward, and waving all the fingers quickly up and down. The reverse of this motion is used for beckoning. Among men the hand-shaking is interminable. A Mexican will keep your hand in his, warmly squeezing it from time to time, while he asks after your health and that of your family, and any question that may occur to him as showing an interest in your welfare. At parting he again seizes it, and holds it while he tries to remember other things he had to say, which will perhaps renew the conversation. Finally, when all topics of interest have been discussed, he will give you a farewell grasp of the hand. If he should meet you a dozen times in the day he will repeat the process. From the President, at the end of an interview, to the shopman, as he hands you the article you have purchased, hand-shaking is almost invariable. It is a sign of intimacy when Mexicans interlock the thumbs in shaking hands. Those who have been separated for some time embrace, and pat each other affectionately on the back. Sometimes one will lift the other up in the exuberance of his joy at the meeting, and it is a comical sight to see the efforts of a small man to lift his taller friend into the air.

If you should express admiration for anything possessed by a Mexican, he will tell you that it is 'muy á la órden,' [1] meaning that it is at your disposal,

---

[1] 'At your orders.'

although, be it remembered, that by this declaration the owner of the coveted article by no means signifies that he expects you to accept it. Another favourite form of speech is used at the parting of persons just introduced. Each will inform the other that he (giving his name) is the servant of his new acquaintance, at whose disposal he places his house at such and such an address. Servants have a curious habit of addressing their mistresses as 'niña,'[1] but the lower orders are very punctilious in addressing each other as Mr., Mrs., or Miss, as the case may be, and speaking of one another as ladies and gentlemen.

A servant will gravely announce the arrival of a 'señora,'[2] who will turn out to be the washerwoman, while a lady friend is spoken of as the 'niña' so and so.

The upper classes in the cities wear European dress, except when riding in the Paseo, where the men appear in the handsome national dress which I have already described. The fashionable young men are as well dressed as any one meets with in London, most of them having their clothes made by the best London tailors, and the ladies frequently have their dresses from Worth.

Foreigners sometimes affect the Mexican dress, but it rarely becomes them; and anything more ridiculous than the appearance of a short, podgy

----

[1] Girl.   [2] A lady.

Englishman in this attire can hardly be imagined. And, with all due respect for the fair sex, I must confess that foreign ladies never look well in a mantilla, nor can they persuade the lace to lie in the graceful folds which seem to fall naturally over the head and shoulders of a Spanish lady. There is a nameless grace which enables those of Spanish origin to wear their dress, and dance their national danza, which no foreigner can successfully imitate.

I ought to say a word about the Mexican blankets, or 'zarapes,' 'jorongos,' or 'cobizas,' as they are called in different parts of the country. They are invaluable, although in a heavy rain I should prefer a suit of Cording's. The blanket is generally about eight feet long by four feet wide, and is made of wool. Those which used to be made in Saltillo were so tightly woven as to be waterproof; but machinery has taken the place of hand-work, and, as often happens, the articles it turns out are far inferior to those which were made before its introduction. These zarapes are woven in different colours, harmoniously blended, and have a slit in the middle, running lengthways, just large enough to put the head through. On horseback the long ends hang so as to cover the rider's legs, while the narrow part protects his chest and back. When on foot this slit is not used; in fact, many are made for pedestrians without it, the zarape being thrown round the body and over the left shoulder. At night it is used as a blanket. I have one in my possession which I prize highly, for it is an old friend, and has often protected me from inclement weather. It is of a kind not often seen, being knitted throughout in soft wool, and I know of nothing so delightfully warm, though it does not weigh four pounds.

The common, half-bred women invariably wear 'rebozos,' [1] which were formerly also made of silk, and worn by ladies. I never see a Mexican girl, with the head and shoulders covered by a rebozo, leaving only the upper part of the face exposed, and carrying her pitcher gracefully poised on her head, without thinking of the Egyptians. I believe that antiquarians are of opinion that these people are descended from that race, and many of the antiquities found in Mexico clearly point in that direction.

These rebozos are used also for carrying babies on the mother's back, this being the reason that so many of the Mexicans turn their toes in, for as infants they are generally carried sitting in the rebozo, with their little feet on either side of the mother's hips.

The national drinks are 'pulque,' 'mezcal,' and 'tequila' on the plateau, and 'aguardiente' and 'habanera' on the lower lands. Pulque is made from the maguey, an aloe plant which covers immense tracts of land, a pulque hacienda [2] yielding rich

---

[1] A long piece of narrow cloth, generally blue, with a fringe, and made of cotton.   [2] Estate.

returns to its owner. The amount that is consumed of this liquor must be prodigious. In the city the pulque shops stand at every corner of the by-streets, and one is aware of their proximity by the horrible pungent odour that issues from these filthy dens, always crowded with customers of the poorest class. It is the every-day drink of the Mexican, and is to be had in the restaurants. Medical men say that it is a very wholesome beverage and an excellent diuretic.

Pulque is like starch in appearance, and emits a peculiar odour not pleasant to the olfactory nerves. That which is sold in the city is stale, and has quite a different taste to pulque when fresh—then it is just drinkable for the newly-arrived foreigner; but it seems horrible stuff in the city. Any one who has to travel in the interior must quickly accustom himself to the national drinks, for in many parts nothing else is to be had, not even water, to quench the thirst. The effect of pulque on those who indulge in it to excess seems to be a stupid drunkenness which the native sleeps off. But if, after a bout at the pulque shop, he adjourns to one of the many canteens attached to the small grocery stores, and drinks some of the fire-water sold in such places, he will become a perfect fiend. An unfortunate gentleman, passing the cathedral one evening, was met by one of these victims of mixed drinks, running amuck with a long knife, and was stabbed to death, though he had never before seen his assassin. The Government strictly

G

enforces the closing of the pulque shops at 7 o'clock in the evening, but allows the much more dangerous canteens to keep open till 12 P.M. Drunkenness is on the increase; and, besides the canteens already spoken of, new drinking saloons are continually being opened for the better classes. In these saloons it is noticeable that the Mexicans now consume their cocktails with as much relish as their northern cousins. Evidently the proprietors of the bar-rooms hope to find their most lucrative custom among the English-speaking part of the community, for every saloon has the words 'Bar-room' or 'Sample-room' inscribed on the doors in large letters.

Tequila is made near Guadalajara, in a town of the same name, from another and smaller aloe. It is a spirit which, in the opinion of many, might be made into an excellent Scotch whisky, if properly prepared so as to have the smoky taste. It is a strong drink; yet in one hot day's ride I have consumed a bottle without feeling any bad effects. The Mexicans call it 'wine,' but it is a rather strong 'wine.' For outward application it is very useful; nothing is more refreshing after a long ride or walk than a tequila bath. By rubbing the spirit well into the body no stiffness will be felt next day. It is the best remedy when mixed with an infusion of tobacco for the poisonous sting of the detestable 'pinolillo' and the 'garrapata.'[1] Mezcal is a somewhat similar drink to tequila.

[1] Insects that make life miserable during the dry months of the year in some parts of the Tropics. It is said that the pinolillo is

The habanera is the favourite drink of the natives of the States of Chiapas, Tabasco, and other hot lands. It is a light rum of pleasant taste, and, if prepared like ordinary rum, would equal the best Jamaica.

Aguardiente is made from the sugar-cane, and is drunk in those districts in which habanera is not made, being much more generally consumed than the latter spirit.

Excellent grapes grow abundantly in many parts of the country, and the wine industry will no doubt eventually receive the attention it merits. The wines now made are of poor quality, and, although they have been extensively advertised, they have not met with much favour.

A capital lager beer is brewed in Toluca by a German, who has had the monopoly of this business for several years and has amassed a considerable fortune. The demand for this beer is always in excess of the supply ; and the brewer has sold out to a wealthy German syndicate, who propose to increase the plant considerably in order to meet the constantly increasing trade.

the young garrapata. The bite of the former causes irritation for weeks afterwards, unless a remedy be applied ; while the garrapata buries its head under the skin. Tequila and tobacco draw it out ; but if the sufferer endeavours to pull it out, it will require a hard pull, taking away part of the skin with it, so tightly does it cling ; and even then the head will remain in, and perhaps cause a boil or at least irritation for long after. The literal translation is an insect which holds on by its legs, and the name is certainly well applied.

CHAPTER VIII

Mexican police—'I'll trouble you for my hat'—Pickpockets and thieves—The 'Ley de fuga'—Diligencia robberies in the olden days—Beggars.

THE police are a courteous and fairly efficient body of men, but their number is too small to enable them to cope properly with the criminal classes of the city and frequent complaints are made in this respect. They generally spend the night-watches in peacefu slumber in sheltering doorways, waking up at the approach of the mounted officer to reply to his questions, and relapsing into the arms of Morpheus when he is safely out of sight. A lantern in the middle of the street at each corner denotes the policeman's presence, and any driver or foot-passenger overturning it is liable to a fine. The policemen of Mexico set an example in politeness to their brethren in New York, and even in London. They are always anxious to be of assistance to the stranger, and will take great pains in directing him to his destination. They are neatly dressed, and a highly respectable-looking set of men. Their arms consist of a staff and a revolver, which they do not hesitate to use on an emergency. In the time of

Gonzalez, an officer of the secret police was one day entering a tramcar when a thief snatched at his hat and ran off with his prize. The officer got down, coolly took aim, and brought his man down with a shot in the leg; he then stepped up to the fallen man, saying, 'I'll trouble you for my hat,' and handed him over to a policeman. It is forbidden to ride at a gallop in the streets of the city, and a policeman will sometimes fire his pistol in the air to stop the offender.

Judicial proceedings are very lengthy, the law allowing so many loopholes, of which the accused can take advantage to delay the course of justice. To cite an example, the man accused in the celebrated 'Rhode murder' case, which caused much sensation, and which happened more than two years ago, has not yet been sentenced, at the time of writing this.

It is said that the 'Ley de fuga'[1] is often employed owing to the delays and uncertainties of the usual legal process. But it is a cruel, arbitrary proceeding. It is applied occasionally to a prisoner while going from one district to another under armed escort. He is told by his guards to go on ahead and then shot in the back, the cause of his death being reported as 'shot while attempting to escape.'

Things have vastly improved since the days of revolutions, when in the disturbed state of the country the interior was infested with men, under the title of

---

[1] Law of flight.

Revolutionaries, who were nothing but highway robbers in organised bands. A body of these men would stop every diligencia as it passed, and their leader would order the passengers to alight. Both the coach and its occupants were minutely searched, every article of any value taken, and the passengers often were stripped of their clothing. This was so frequently done that at the inns and halfway houses stores of paper were always kept to supply the lack of necessary garments.

The beggars in the capital are as the sands on the sea-shore, and the appearance of their vermin-covered bodies, barely concealed by filthy rags, is most repulsive. Distorted arms and legs, and every monstrous deformity, are seen on all sides. Every period of life is represented—from the child hardly able to walk to the helpless aged—all with the same prayer for a little alms, ' Por el amor de Dios,'[1] which is met by a polite request to be pardoned ' for the love of God ' when the person addressed has no alms to give ; and, indeed, the patient, suppliant look which the beggar assumes makes it hard to refuse his request.

[1] ' For the love of God.'

CHAPTER IX

Mexican currency — Mexican millionaires — Principal export — Mexican fruits—Mexico as a field for investment.

MEXICAN currency, till lately, consisted of bank-bills in denominations of from 1 dollar to 1,000 dollars, silver dollars, 50 cents, 25 cents, 12½ cents (reals), 6¼ cents (medios, or half reals), 10 cents, and 5 cent pieces, the copper coins being cents and 'tlacos' (1½ cent). These cents were often cut in half to facilitate change in small transactions. Roughly speaking, a dollar is worth 3s. 6d., and a real 5¼d. During the presidency of Gonzalez nickel five-cent pieces were issued, but as these were used in the most unscrupulous manner by men of wealth and position, who enriched themselves by buying the coins as they arrived from abroad, where they had been minted, at a heavy discount, the result was the 'Nickel Riot,' which came near assuming formidable proportions.

The discontent was so general and so freely expressed that it was not to be treated with contempt, and finally the nickels were withdrawn from circulation. On the accession of Diaz he abolished the tlacos, a measure which also caused some discontent, but as it was carried out judiciously, it occasioned no disturbance. Later on an edict was published to the effect that all reals and half-real pieces in circulation must be exchanged for their face value, in coins of the decimal system, by July 1, 1890. This had long been necessary; these coins were the remnant of the old system, and many were so worn that people began to refuse to take them, as the inscriptions had entirely disappeared, their value being thereby much depreciated, in addition to the loss caused by having the two systems of coinage current at the same time.

The designs of the Mexican coins are not intricate, especially that of the dollar, which is very crude; but this cannot be altered, for the Chinese, who use the Mexican dollar largely in their country, as being the purest silver coin in existence, and to whom millions are exported yearly, would not accept them if the design were changed. As a result, they are easily imitated, the metal used being tin, lead, or copper, and the imitations are often so good as to be difficult to detect.

Although the natives rarely take a coin without biting and ringing it, there is an enormous amount of false money in circulation, and the coiners are rarely captured. In a country where the means of communication have hitherto been so few, the rates of exchange between towns in the interior and the capital are necessarily high, as the cost of remitting funds between places off the railroads is heavy. The national banks charged ½ to 5 per cent. for exchanges and on their bank-notes issued by branch offices in the interior, but, with the increased railroad communication, there is now really no excuse for this, so far as those towns are concerned through which the railroads pass. The Bank of London and South America has scored a point in the public favour by paying its branch bank-bills without discount.

Among the Mexicans are many men of great wealth, derived almost entirely from estates and landed property, a large proportion of the principal mines being owned by foreigners. There are men such as the Iturbes, who own not only the Iturbide Hotel, but the whole of the block in which it stands, including the San Carlos, another large hotel, and numerous shops and houses, which alone yield an enormous income, apart from other large estates belonging to this wealthy family, whose administrator has become one of the richest men in the capital. There are many others who derive large incomes from city property, while many of the hacendados[1] in the interior are enormously rich. The largest fortunes made of late years have been derived from the henequen, or sisal hemp, so-called from its having been originally exported from the Port of Sisal, now discarded for that of Progreso. These henequen estates are mines of gold for their lucky proprietors. The plant requires little attention or labour, and the cost

---

[1] Owners of estates.

of production of the hemp is infinitely small as compared with the price that it obtains. In Merida, the
capital of Yucatan, where all the henequen hacendados
reside, a man's income is calculated at so much per
diem. There are men who are worth 500 dollars and
1,000 dollars a day, while a daily revenue of 200 or
300 dollars is thought little of. Yet many of these
people live very simply, spending little except on
their European tours, when they are extravagant in
their tastes. Next in importance are the pulque
haciendas, which are of great extent and yield princely
revenues. The sugar estates are also sources of great
wealth, and machinery of the most improved kind is
frequently used. I have known as much as 250,000
dollars paid for a new plant in one case.

America absorbs nearly all the henequen produced
for her rope and other fibre manufactures, but hardly
any sugar is exported. The principle upon which the
sugar and coffee hacendados conduct their business
appears to be to grow only sufficient for the demands
of the neighbourhood of their estates, and for this purpose they keep shops in the nearest large town, where
they sell it to the small dealers. As the tariff is so
high as to be prohibitory to the importation of foreign
sugars, they can obtain highly remunerative prices;
and it is a fact that poorly-refined sugar costs in
Mexico more than good loaf-sugar fetches in London.
I had a curious instance of this anomaly when visiting
Uruapam, on the Pacific slopes, then a two-days' ride

from the terminus of the National Railway. The coffee produced in this neighbourhood is delicious, being considered by many to be equal to the finest Mocha. After getting the lowest obtainable price, I sent samples to a firm of London brokers, who classed it as first-rate, quoting as the London market rate a price slightly inferior to that which I had been asked on the plantations.

Cattle is another great source of wealth in the interior, where there are large 'potreros,' in which the cattle are fattened upon Para, or Guinea grass, that grows in great abundance and fattens the animals very quickly.

But the profits which the Mexican millionaires derive from these and other sources are of little advantage to the country, for, with all their wealth, they mostly spend little on living, or in purchase of commodities sold in the country. Their horses are of American or English breed, and their carriages are made by the best Long Acre or Paris manufacturers. Their clothes they bring, to a great extent, from Europe, and they spend their money when engaged on European tours.

The exports of the country are chiefly bullion and silver, henequen, mahogany, cedar and dye-woods, tobacco and cigars, coffee, hides, ixtle,[1] zacaton,[2] goatskins, india-rubber, and chicle or chewing gum, fruit, vanilla, &c.

[1] A kind of hemp.   [2] A coarse fibre used for brushes, mats, &c.

It is said that the Cuban manufacturers, who meet with much difficulty in finding labour, now that the slaves have been emancipated, are carefully examining the tobacco districts of Mexico, with a view to transferring their industry to that country. Be this as it may, there is no doubt that Mexican cigars are meeting with increased favour, and the future of this industry is a very bright one. All along the coasts are tracts of land where the soil is eminently adapted for tobacco growing. I have bought cigars near Tuxpam at 1 dollar 25 cents per hundred, or, say, $\frac{1}{2}d.$ apiece, which could not be equalled in London under $4d.$

There are a number of houses that make cigarettes, but they are not careful that the quality should always remain the same. A new brand will be put on the market, and, as soon as it has found favour, the quality becomes poorer, and it gradually falls out of use.

The coffee growing is done principally by the Indians on their little plantations, and the machinery used is of a most primitive kind.

Great quantities of sugar are made throughout the lower parts of the country. Some of the richest lands on the Pacific are, however, in such unhealthy districts that large haciendas are lying idle and valueless. But this will be soon remedied, for the Chinese, who are now deprived of the outlet for their surplus population which America afforded them, have cast their eyes on Mexico, and wealthy Chinese syndicates have secured important concessions from the Government, with a view to the emigration of their countrymen to the Pacific slopes.

'Zacaton' has only been exported of late years, and there is a continually increasing demand for this useful fibre. It is said to have been first discovered by a Frenchman, who collected it with his own hands until he had made sufficient, by the sale of a few bales in Europe, to enable him to employ labour. As its value was then unknown, he was allowed to collect it wherever he liked, until his exportations had become so considerable that the attention of others was directed to it. By that time he had realised a comfortable competence, on which he retired to his native land.

'Chicle' is another product that has only attracted attention for the last few years. It is now exported largely to the States, where the ridiculous practice of chewing gum seems to have become almost universal lately among women and children. It is extracted from a tree bearing that name, which grows wild in the vicinity of Tuxpam and Tampico, simply by tapping the tree with a stroke of the machete,[1] and collecting the white liquid, which flows in a vessel, and boiling it into a compact mass, when it is ready for exportation.

In view of the ever-increasing demand for india-

---

[1] A short sword.

rubber, attention is being paid to its cultivation in
Mexico, and some plantations of trees have been laid
out, but not nearly on the scale required. This is
one of the most promising products of the country,
and, when properly developed, it will be a very
valuable article of export, having the advantage of
requiring little labour and attention, and producing
abundant yields. It is drawn from the trees in the
same way as the chicle, and prepared for exportation
by mixing with it the sap of a certain creeper found
in the woods, which solidifies the rubber. The trees
should not be tapped before they are seven years old,
after which, with proper treatment, they will bear for
ever.

Mexico produces fruits of all kinds, and of the
most delicious flavour—apples, pears, cherries, plums,
peaches, nectarines, walnuts, peanuts, grapes, &c.,
grow in abundance on the table-land ; while oranges,
pineapples, bananas, mangoes, cherimoyas, guavas,
coyol, zapote, limes, lemons, anonas, aguacate, and a
host of others, grow in the Tropics.

With such an abundance of fruit and sugar it is
surprising that, as yet, no fruit-canning industry has
been started, with the exception of one manufactory
recently established by some enterprising Americans
in Ensenada, Lower California. It is a positive fact
that in some of the woods of the hacienda which I
visited, and of which I shall speak later on, the lemons
and oranges lie so thick that it is dangerous to ride

through them, so slippery is the ground with rotting fruit; yet on that same hacienda a glass of lemonade was a luxury, because, forsooth, sugar was dear.

Vanilla grows principally on a narrow belt of land in the Papantla district, near Tuxpam, and is cultivated by the Indians who are so fortunate as to possess land in this district. They are the richest tribe in Mexico, and well they may be, when as much as ten dollars per hundred is paid for the vanilla beans. All the women wear a profusion of heavy gold ornaments. There is no doubt that all along this part of the coast there is land suitable for the cultivation of this valuable plant, and the owners of property in the neighbourhood are rapidly becoming more alive to its value.

Those who have not travelled through the country can form no conception of how marvellously rich it is. Although one of the oldest countries in the world, it is in its infancy as regards the development of its resources; and now that Mexico City can be easily reached in twelve days from London and five days from New York, investors can have more control over their affairs there than has hitherto been possible. The success of the English companies already started, and the dividends they have paid, show clearly what an advantageous field for enterprise Mexico has proved herself to be; and it is safe to predict that she will some day, not far distant, be more prosperous than the Argentine Republic in its palmiest days. Her proximity to the principal markets of the world, the uninterrupted peace she is enjoying, her following wisely in the steps of her sister Republic, the United States, in minding her own business, together with her solid Government and un-rivalled riches, must insure for her a brilliant future.

CHAPTER X

Tramcars—Cabs—Lighting of streets—Telegraphs and telephones—
Luxurious railroad travelling—Railway extensions—Mexico's
improved communications—The Post Office—Improvements in
the city—Progress of the country—President Diaz—System
of taxation.

IT seems hard to believe that not twenty-five years
ago the only kind of conveyance in Mexico was that
clumsy old stage-coach, which one sees lumbering
over the pavement every day, now used for carrying
the mail from the station to the Post Office. Look at
the city to-day. The Zocalo is a labyrinth of rails,
radiating to every point of the compass, and thirty or
forty neat cars, with well-fed mules, may be counted
any day waiting the hour for starting.

The Tramcar Company is one of the best managed
and best paying concerns in the country. It owns
over three hundred first and second-class cars—all
imported from the United States—which in the year
1888 conveyed over sixteen millions of passengers,
according to its traffic returns.

Another company has also been formed for cars
with steam traction, to compete with the old company,

H

so far as some of the suburbs are concerned. The line is finished and everything is ready for opening, so that the suburban residents are to be congratulated upon the additional facilities that they will enjoy shortly, and there will be, no doubt, quite an exodus from the city in consequence.

The cabs are all numbered and divided into four classes, distinguishable by the colour of a little metal flag, which stands at the driver's side when his cab is for hire. The green-flag cabs are entitled to charge $1 50 cents per hour, the blue $1, the red 75 cents, and the white 50 cents.

The principal streets and squares of the city are lighted by electricity, and a good many shops have incandescent lamps. Gas is used in all the other streets, except on the outskirts, where oil lamps hang on wires across the road.

Besides the Central and National Railroads, which receive telegrams at their offices, there are three other telegraph offices in the city ; and messages may be sent to all parts of the world by the Submarine Cable Company.

There is also a Telephone Company, which has a large number of subscribers not only in the city but in the suburbs, and is a great convenience.

The stations of the railroad companies are all on the outskirts of the city, this being the rule throughout the Republic ; in fact, in most parts of the interior they are at such a distance from the towns as to require tramcars or carriages to convey passengers to their homes.

The Central and National Railroad Companies are eagerly competing for the overland travel, and passengers can enjoy the luxuries of Pullman and buffet cars, and even vestibuled trains, on the trip from Mexico to New York. The National advertises the journey in the 'Aztec Limited' to New York in five days, while the Central is little behind its rival in the matter of time, with its splendidly-equipped 'Moctezuma' vestibuled train, besides having the advantage of the broad gauge.

These vestibuled trains have reduced the discomforts of railway travelling to a minimum. They consist of a drawing-room, library, smoking-room, dining-room, and dormitory cars, the latter being supplied with bath-rooms, hot and cold water, &c. The library cars have a liberal supply of standard works, the drawing-rooms are luxuriously furnished, and excellent meals are supplied in the buffet cars.

A comparison of Mexico as I found it on my arrival, with its present condition, in the matter of means of communication, will give some idea of the wonderfully rapid progress the country is making. At that time the only communication that Mexico had with the outer world was by the Mexican Railway to Vera Cruz, whence steamers sailed weekly to New York, and monthly by the Royal Mail Line to Southampton, or by the Transatlantique Company's steamers to France. Now there are daily mails; letters, which before took thirty days, now only require sixteen to reach England, and even less. The steamship lines have been improved greatly. The comfortable old steamers of the Alexandre Line between Vera Cruz and New York have been bought by the Ward Company, who have refitted them with new engines, refurnished and redecorated them throughout, and reduced the time occupied in the trip. The French line has transferred some of its large steamers to Vera Cruz, making the journey to France in seventeen days; while the Spanish Transatlantic Company has established a service between Mexico and the Spanish and French ports, in splendidly equipped steamers.

It is a great pity that the Royal Mail Company discontinued their service in 1888, just at the time when the French and Spanish Companies were beginning to develop the trade; for if, instead of withdrawing its steamers, larger and more commodious vessels had been put on the line, and more attention had been paid to increased facilities for passengers and shippers, there can be no doubt that it would have shared in the prosperity its former competitors now enjoy.

A glance at the map of Mexico will show what great strides have been made during the last five years, since the first railway to connect Mexico with the United States was completed. The Central Rail-

way, built with capital supplied by wide-awake
Bostonians, has since then, under its present able
management, been greatly improved. Its weak
points have everywhere been carefully strengthened,
and the wash-outs, which so frequently intercepted
communication, in one case for as much as a fort-
night, now rarely occur. To-day it is as well built
and managed a line as almost any in the States; its
revenues steadily increase, and it is considered a first-
class investment. The extension to Guadalajara on
the Pacific side, and through San Luis Potosi to
Tampico on the Gulf Coast, has opened up some of
the richest agricultural parts of the country, and
when the cutting of Tampico Bar has been completed, Mexico will, for the first time, be supplied
with an excellent harbour on the Gulf side, in which
a fleet can lie in safety, and Tampico will become the
principal seaport of the Republic. Besides the advantage which Tampico can offer as a port, its
position insures its future, being nearest to the
American shores, and in a direct line with San Blas
on the Pacific, with which it will soon be in communication by the railway, part of which is already
finished, between Guadalajara and that port. San
Luis Potosi must, from its situation, almost in the
centre of the country, soon absorb much of the
trade; and the greater part of the merchandise must
pass through Tampico, which will shortly have
another railway, the Monterey and Gulf, which,

starting from Monterey and passing through some of the most fertile lands of Mexico and Ciudad Victoria, a town of considerable importance, will give a much shorter route from the port.

The National Railroad was completed to the frontier only two years ago, and was the first to place San Luis Potosi in communication with Mexico City; it has also extended its line from Morelia to Patzcuaro, and will eventually continue its rails to the Pacific port of Mazatlan. Five years ago the Interoceanic Railroad was a dream. The Mexican Railroad Company, in the fancied security of the concession originally granted them by the Government, which was believed to grant them virtually the monopoly of the route to Vera Cruz, were surprised one day to learn that Don Delfin Sanchez, an enterprising Spaniard, at that time owner of a small local railroad running from the capital to Cuautla, had obtained a concession to continue his railway to Vera Cruz and to Acapulco, on the Pacific side. The news was scarcely credited at first, but it was soon learned that an English company had been formed, with ample capital to carry out the new undertaking, and before the surprise had died out engineers were already at work, and before the publication of this book the line will be completed to Vera Cruz. So far the competition has only affected the old company at Puebla, through which both lines pass, resulting in a reduction of the first-class fares by one-half; but

its effects must be felt to Vera Cruz. However, the
Interoceanic is a narrow gauge, and has been unfortunate in having suffered several breakdowns at
first, which has prejudiced the public somewhat
against it, although no serious accident has happened. Still, by the time it is completed to the
port, and has reduced the rates considerably, as it
undoubtedly will, of the Mexican Railroad, these little
incidents will have been forgotten ; and it remains
to be seen whether or not the country traversed by
these two railways, and the commerce of Mexico, can
support them both. The Interoceanic Railroad is
already looking towards the extension of the line to
its other objective point, Acapulco, so that here again
is the probability of the early completion of another
railway across the Mexican Republic.

Meanwhile the Mexican Company has not been
idle, and has extended a branch from the main line
to Pachuca. This thriving town, one of the principal mining centres of the country, in which a colony
of Cornishmen are rapidly making money, will soon
have no less than three railways, and will be connected with Tuxpam and Tampico by a road being built
by an English company to those ports. Another most
important railway is now being rapidly constructed,
starting from Puebla, which will also soon be quite a
railroad centre, and traversing the State of Oaxaca,
the mineral riches of which are well known, and
which is also a most fertile State. This road, also the

property of an English company, and which is named
the Southern Pacific Company, will meet the Pacific
Railroad that is being built across the southern part
of Mexico, having for its termini Tonalá on the Gulf
coast and Puerto Angel on the Pacific, traversing the
rich and little-known States of Tabasco and Chiapas,
where one of the richest mines in the world has
recently been found, thus forming a third trans-
continental route. The South Pacific will bring the
capital to within a short distance of the Guatemalan
frontier, and will, jointly with the Central, form part
of the line by which it is proposed to connect the
United States with all South America—an ambitious
scheme which has every probability of accomplishment.

It will be seen that the railroad system is now
practically in the hands of English bondholders, for
in addition to the lines built, and in course of construction, with English capital, the greater part of
the stock of the Central and National Railway, which
was constructed to a considerable extent with American money, is now held by the English.

While a great network of railways has been
formed in such a short space of time, the Post Office
has not been behind-hand. Eight years ago any one
desirous of mailing a letter had to deposit it with the
post-office clerk with twenty-five cents in payment of
postage, as no stamps were sold to the public. There
was one small dark office in which the public mailed
or received its letters, and another little den where a

spectacled, suspicious old gentleman received or delivered registered packets. Now the rates have been reduced to five cents for 'the United States and Canada, and ten cents for any other part of the world, which amount, curiously enough, is charged for all letters to the interior of the country. The large Patio has been converted into a fine hall, in which are the post-office boxes, some two hundred in number, the stamp office, &c., while all round the wall are slabs of onyx for the use of those desirous of writing.

Mexico City, too, has wonderfully improved during these few years; her streets, then paved with cobbles or uneven blocks of stones, are now laid down with wood or asphalte. Huge pumps now empty her streets within a short time of the waters that formerly flooded them for hours after a heavy shower; her Alameda has been converted from a wilderness to a lovely park, her squares have been laid out in pretty gardens, handsome new houses have been built, and the value of property has risen enormously. The drainage of the valley, the most important need of all, has been taken in hand and energetically pushed forward, and Mexico will shortly be supplied with a perfect system.

Such is briefly the progress that has been made in this short period. For this, and for the continued prosperity of the country, and its high credit abroad, Mexico must thank her present broad-minded, far-seeing ruler, Porfirio Diaz, who was accused at one time of bringing his country to the verge of bankruptcy by offering so many concessions for the construction of railroads. Instead of bankruptcy he has, by his wise and beneficent measures, brought his country to a height of prosperity never dreamed of; and his countrymen cannot be sufficiently grateful for all he has done.

The banks are prospering, and have during the last two or three years opened branches in the most important cities; new banks have sprung up in the capital and elsewhere, new railroads have been pushed forward in all directions, and a fine new harbour will soon be opened. Diaz, besides being a statesman of high order, who has known how to attract to his support the most able men in the country for his Government, is a soldier, and rules Mexico with a firm hand. Now, with the great railroad facilities, he can mass troops anywhere with the greatest ease, and revolutions, as in the days of old, are no longer possible, any attempt at a political movement being promptly crushed, often without the public knowing anything of it. No mercy is shown to the leaders of such attempts, and he would be a bold man who attempted to disturb the present peace of the country. The President has earned for himself the respect of all, not only as a ruler but as a private citizen. He is a gentleman of most polished manners, a good husband and father; his mode of life is simple and unostentatious, and he has a high reputation for probity. He is a great friend of the foreigner, whose aid he is anxious to enlist in the development of his country, and is always willing to lend a ready ear for any scheme which will tend to its advancement.

One of Mexico's greatest drawbacks is her system of taxation, and the heavy expense of her Government. The ambition of every Mexican appears to be to obtain a post in the civil service, and to this is due the bribery and extortion so frequent. Taxation falls heaviest on the commercial classes, and, consequently, upon the foreigner. The system of collection is radically bad. Taxes have to be paid at the Government office, no reminder being sent as to the days they fall due ; but if not paid by that date a prompt notice is despatched calling for the payment of the tax in the term of three or four days, plus 10 per cent. for collection and sundry other charges.

In the taxation of business houses the merchants have to make a declaration of their capital and sales in the year. This is referred to a jury, who decide as to the quota which is to be imposed. The landlord pays taxes on his property only when occupied or cultivated. The large property holders, many of whom own estates of fifty and sixty square leagues in extent, seem to neglect their property in order to escape heavy taxation.

CHAPTER XI

The Mexican character—Mexican hospitality—Their universal
courtesy—Their fondness of music—Half-breeds and Indians—
Indians and their religion—The warlike tribes—The padre out-
witted by the Indian—Tact and patience necessary in dealing
with all classes.

I ONCE asked an English gentleman, who had lived in
Mexico all his life, to define the Mexican character.
He smilingly declined the difficult task. The aptest
definition that I have heard was that given me
by one Mexican when speaking of another: he described him as 'algo de todo'—somewhat of everything. Speaking generally, they are an intelligent,
courteous, and diplomatic race, fond of their families,
and suspicious of foreigners, indolent, and given to
procrastination, the upper classes fond of outward
show, while the lower orders are contented with little.
All are proud of their country and jealous of outside
interference. They are critical and conservative,
more given to speech than to action; jealous, and
often revengeful and cruel; susceptible to kindness,
yet obstinate under harsh treatment; apt learners and
good imitators. With politeness, tact, firmness, and
justice much may be done with a Mexican; but he

resents keenly rude and arbitrary treatment. Much has been said of their hospitality; but they are careful not to introduce the foreigner into their family circle. An invitation to dine at a Mexican house is exceedingly rare. On the other hand, an acquaintance, dining at the same restaurant with you, will sometimes quietly pay your bill and his too, the waiter's reply when you ask for your account being ' Está pagado.' [1] They rarely entertain in the usual sense of giving dances or dinner parties; but occasionally a few bachelor friends will be invited to a dinner at a restaurant or Tivoli. On these occasions nothing is too good nor too expensive, and a plentiful repast is served, which lasts many hours.

The foreigner cannot fail to be struck with the universal courtesy. A poor workman will raise his hat with native grace to any female acquaintance, and often to those of his own sex, and will ask the customary questions as to the health of the family, &c., with as much courtesy as the highest in the land.

All the polite expressions are as common with them as among the upper classes, and they are always willing to help each other. It is rare to see a child beaten or crying. The little ones all seem to inherit their parents' blissful contentedness. Everywhere the innate politeness of all who have Spanish blood in their veins is evident, and any omission of the polite

---

[1] 'It is paid.'

forms of speech is looked upon as showing want of breeding.

Many of the young men of good family have received a college education in England. Students in Mexico are very intelligent, but I think the knowledge they acquire is often superficial.

The contentment of the lower orders is the bane of Mexico. It is this which makes it so difficult to get work out of them. If they had ambition, a desire to make money in order to improve their position, to dress better, to educate their families, &c., the labour problem of Mexico could be more easily solved, although the greatest difficulty lies in the lack of population. The aim of the Mexican workman appears to be to earn a little money, sufficient to supply him with his tortillas and frijoles, an occasional bull-fight, or a little drinking or gambling. He then has no desire to work until his money is exhausted. Hence, if anything is required to be done, the word 'mañana' springs to their lips, meaning literally 'to-morrow,' but practically 'at some more convenient season.' Untruthfulness is universal among the lower orders; and in the capital they are nearly all petty thieves. They steal small articles which are not likely to be missed, and in purchasing at the market the servant invariably pays one price and charges his mistress another.

Few people are more fond of music; it is a poor house in a large city that cannot boast of its piano;

and 'Pleyel,' 'Erard,' 'Steinway,' 'Collard,' and other good makes are met with, very good instruments being also made by Germans in the capital. The ladies play with execution and feeling, but singing is rarely heard in the cities. Rich and poor are alike fond of music. Their regimental bands are excellent, and even small towns have music in the Plaza once or twice a week. A pleasant accompaniment to a dance or dinner party is the music of stringed instruments—guitars, violas, violins; and I know no music more pleasant to dance to. In the interior, guitars and violins are very general, and the natives have a number of airs which are always of a melancholy kind. The men sing, or rather howl, choruses which are not by any means musical or pleasing to the ear.

As musical critics the educated Mexicans excel. Woe to the tenor who is not in voice, or the orchestra if it is below par! Patti confessed that she never felt so nervous as at her first appearance before a Mexican audience, and it is said that at the commencement of her singing some hisses were heard, which were, however, succeeded by rapturous applause. Rarely, perhaps, has she had such an ovation as when she sang 'Home, Sweet Home' in Mexico City.

Among the educated classes are to be found some men of enterprise and ambition, notably the President, General Pacheco, who, although he has lost an arm and a leg in the service of his country, is one of the most active and hardworking men in the Republic, and to whose encouragement much of the foreign enterprise is due; Sr. Camacho, who is actively interested in the Central Railroad; Salvador Malo, the concessionaire of the Monte de Piedad Bank scheme; Sr. Guzman, the originator of the Tramcar Company, and many others; but, generally speaking, the indolence of the Mexicans is proverbial—fond of theories which they will propound with great volubility, they prefer looking on and criticising while others work. Their conversational powers are wonderful. I have heard two gentlemen talking almost without cessation in the train all the way from Vera Cruz to Mexico, a journey which occupies thirteen hours.

Many of the half-breeds and Indians are cruel. This is apparent in the sore backs of their unhappy beasts of burden, which would make the hairs of a member of the S.P.C.A. stand on end. An attempt has been made to found a society for the protection of animals, but without success. What chance of existence could such an institution have in a country where bull-fighting is sanctioned by law and society? But the native seems to be cruel from birth. Children will amuse themselves by torturing any little animal that they have caught, while the men are ingenious in the tortures they inflict on their fellow-beings. When an unfortunate peon is attacked by thieves who are not satisfied with the plunder found upon him, they have been known to leave him bound to a tree, exposed to the fierce rays of the sun, after having beaten him almost to death; or they may pare the flesh from the feet of their victim and drive him before them till he drops.

Every attempt is being made to educate the lower orders. Schools are to be found in all the little towns, and the scholars appear to be studious and well-behaved. The Mexican boy is the reverse of our English lad. Mischief never seems to come into his head, and a smile rarely crosses his face. From the age of three or four years, children are inured to fatigue. Often a little man may be seen, who can hardly toddle, carrying a bundle as big as himself, or accompanying his father to his day's work in the field, while the girls at five or six years of age can make tortillas and prepare the meals as well as their mothers.

The climate and district largely influence the character. It will be found invariably that the less the altitude the more pleasant and natural are the natives. It is on the plateau that the melancholy faces and disposition so general among the inhabitants of Mexico are especially noticeable. One of the things that most strikes a visitor is the impassiveness of the faces he sees around him. They might be called almost devoid of expression were it not for the dark, bead-like eyes that nothing escapes, and which light up with an evil glitter when the passions are aroused. Authors trace this melancholy of the people to the

I

effects of the Spanish Conquest. This may have been
originally the cause ; but there can be no doubt that
the frequency of the revolutions, in which the poor
always suffered, their little all being taken to feed the
bands of organised robbers who scoured the country,
while each successive Government ground them down
unmercifully with taxations and extortion of every
kind, and the cruel treatment they have suffered at
the hands of their masters, the hacendados, who only
looked upon them as slaves, have combined to mould
the character of the people and give them an appearance of resignation as though ' Kismet ' were written
on their faces.   As a matter of fact the poor peon
becomes a slave of the estate.   As soon as the peons
owe the owner money—and they can only obtain the
few things they require at the hacienda store on
credit—they are slaves until their indebtedness is
paid off with labour.   I knew one man who borrowed
from his master twenty-five dollars, to repay which
he had to work eighteen hours a day for seven
months.

The half-breeds are more sickly than the Indians,
owing to their constitutions being weakened by a
vicious life and impure blood handed down from
generations.   Their method of living is not in any
way conducive to morality, health, and cleanliness.

The hacendados generally look to the half-breeds
for the defence of the estates in case of an attack,
the Indians not being, as a rule, good fighters.   The

half-breeds are generally called 'gente de razon,' [1] or 'Christians,' though few of them have any right to either qualification.   They are the storekeepers in small villages and ranches, their methods of calculation and system of weights and measures being generally ruinous to their more ignorant Indian customers.

Between the half-breeds and Indians there is little sympathy; in fact, if the truth were known, the latter hate the gente de razon cordially.

Of the character and habits of the Indians little is known; when there are so many tribes, speaking dialects unintelligible to each other, and spread over so large a territory, and living, as they do, apart from the half-breeds, they can only be judged by outward appearances, and such limited experience as one may have had of them when travelling.   Their expression is heavy and stolid, the complexion varying from copper colour to white.   Generally the nose is rather flat, the upper lip broad and straight from the nose, the eyes black, and the forehead low and fringed with long coarse black hair.   The dress is picturesque, but almost invariably ragged and filthy.   The women sometimes wear necklaces of amber, or other ornaments, round the neck, and both sexes are fond of wearing charms.   In Yucatan and other parts of the Tropics they are scrupulously clean in their apparel, and I have noticed that the greater the altitude the

[1] Educated people.

dirtier the Indians.   In the capital they are worse in
this respect than anywhere; their scanty rags are
disgusting to look at, and their bodies are covered
with vermin.   Their idea of religion amounts to
idolatry; but their priests, for whom they profess the
greatest reverence, have to be very careful with them.
I knew one curiosity-hunter, who had bought from
the priest of a village some fine old embroideries;
but the Indians got wind of it, and, armed with
clubs, attacked the purchaser, who was glad to get
away alive, leaving his spoil behind him.   A priest
near Orizaba was cut to pieces for having given
serious offence to his Indian parishioners.   Nor can
their saints always depend upon good treatment at their
hands.   The image of the Virgin was once brought
out by some Indians and implored for rain.   No rain
fell, however, and the unfortunate Virgin was set upon
and broken into a thousand fragments.

Most of the tribes are peaceful and harmless, but
others are warlike and indomitable.

The Yaquis, a remarkably fine race, many of whom
stand nearly seven feet in height, give constant trouble
to the Government, and, as a matter of fact, are never
subdued.   Yucatan is peopled by a wild race, which
the Government never attempts to subjugate.   In
this province the only towns where any but Indians
can live are Progreso, the port, and Merida, the
capital, distant from the former only a few miles;
and it is only of late that their inhabitants have felt

any security from the raids which used to be made by these barbarians. The rest of this province, stretching inland, is entirely unexplored. Wondrous tales are told of beautiful cities, and other fables; but no white man who has attempted to go into the interior has ever been known to come back alive, although its exploration has often been undertaken, and by considerable numbers of armed men.

The Indians of Mexico have rites of their own, and customs of which the half-breeds know nothing. They possess secrets which would be invaluable to the world at large, could they be induced to divulge them. They have infallible remedies for diseases which puzzle our most learned medical men, and poisons and antidotes of all kinds. The unfortunate ex-Empress Carlotta, widow of Maximilian, is said to have been poisoned by an Indian herb, which induces dementia by slow degrees. But there is no remedy for it known to science, though, probably, the Indians have the antidote. They know where precious metals and stones are to be found, and where treasures lie buried, hidden by their ancestors from the greed of the Spanish conquerors, but their secrets are never revealed.

There is no more suspicious or secretive character in the world than the Mexican Indian. This is so much the case that even the Indian women married to half-breeds never disclose to their husbands any of the secrets of their tribe. Each little community is ruled by a 'Regidor,' who appears to use considerable tact in dealing with those whom he has been elected to rule. If Indians are required to work they must first be treated with, and they must then get the consent of their people before anything is settled.

In dealing with the natives of Mexico, whether half-breeds or Indians, the utmost tact and patience are necessary. Their modes of thinking and doing things are entirely different to our notions; in fact, they seem to do everything in a manner opposite to that which common sense would dictate. With proper management much can be done with them.

In dealing with the educated classes especially, politeness and tact are necessary. In Government and in legal matters it is always best to place the matter in the hands of the most influential representative and the best lawyer to be found, and then fortify one's self with patience.

When pricing an article, to offer a fraction of what is asked, and if the offer be refused to turn on the heel and walk away, is useless. The seller will not call you back. But if you are willing to spend a quarter of an hour in gravely discussing the matter, pointing out the defects of the article, mentioning incidentally the prices you have previously paid, &c., the probability is you will win the day. And so it is in all dealings with the Mexicans; impatience or loss of temper will often defeat a purpose which, with a little diplomacy, might easily be effected. At any rate, this has been my experience.

CHAPTER XII

Religion in Mexico—The Reform Laws and the English bishop—The influence of the clergy—Mexican churches—Foreign missions—The Episcopal Church—The American hospital—Christenings, weddings, and burials—Church festivals—The Passion Play in Mexico—The Carnival — The legend of Nuestra Señora de Guadalupe.

THE Roman Catholic religion holds a powerful sway in the country, though considerably shorn of its attributes by the Reform Laws. Priests are forbidden to wear any distinctive garb in the streets, and open-air religious processions are forbidden under pain of heavy fines. Yet so great is the hold of religion over the Indians that the inhabitants of a village will club together to make up the amount of the fine sooner than be deprived of their procession on saints' days. These constantly recurring feast days are a great drawback to Mexico's progress—as, indeed, they are in all Spanish-speaking countries. Every great saint's day—and their name is legion—means a total stoppage of labour, not only for the day, but often for the next, when the votaries of religion are getting over the effects of the holiday.

An amusing instance of the strictness with which

the Reform Laws are enforced in the city occurred a few years ago. An English bishop who was visiting the city issued from his hotel in full Episcopalian garb—shovel hat, gaiters, &c. A policeman at once stepped up to him, and, informing him that his garb was against the law, requested him to return and assume a layman's dress. His lordship was so infuriated at this meddling with his attributes, that he took train for Vera Cruz the following morning and left the country.

The further one goes from the seat of Government the power of the priests becomes more noticeable, and even in some large towns in the interior they openly infringe the laws of the country. In many parts the people are very bigoted, and the influence of the clergy over the women is boundless. There are rich ladies who never take any step in their temporal matters without first consulting their spiritual advisers. They always wear mantillas when going to Mass, it being considered disrespectful to appear in the house of God in a hat or bonnet. While visiting a church in Morelia a verger stepped up to us and politely recommended my wife to leave, as her bonnet was not a becoming head-dress. Morelia is a very bigoted town, and I must say that this is the only case of its kind that I have heard of among foreign visitors.

After the beauties of the Spanish and other European churches, those of Mexico are very disappointing. It is true that revolutions have despoiled them of the riches which they formerly owned, for, after the Spanish Conquest, no paintings were too good, embroideries too rich, or jewellery too valuable for the Spanish magnates to bring to the churches of their adopted country. The façades of many of the Mexican churches are very fine, and adorned with much rich carving in wood and stone; but their interior decoration is generally of a tawdry description, and often in sad want of repair. That of the cathedral in the city of Mexico leaves much to be desired in point of artistic decoration, but there are some fine paintings, and the carving is very handsome. The exterior is grand, and, viewed by moonlight, the quaint, irregular pile, part built of granite and part of red sandstone, adorned with rich carvings, and surmounted by the grand old towers, has an enchanting effect.

The revenues of the Church are, to a great extent, derived from the poor, who sacrifice much for the priests. The fact of there being so many illegitimate children is attributed in a great measure to the exorbitant marriage fees; and it is said that no small part of the income of the priests is produced by the sale of the unconsumed tapers, which are resold to the candle-makers.

There is absolute freedom of religion under the Reform Laws of Mexico, and the country is flooded with Baptist and other Dissenting missionaries, who, although protected by the laws in the large towns, often get into trouble in the interior; and occasionally we hear of a mission being attacked and its occupants being obliged to flee for their lives. When we arrived the only place of worship for Episcopalians was in a little bare room, in which a devoted old English gentleman had read the service to a congregation of five or ten people for several years. Later on, the English colony subscribed for a clergyman's salary, and a suitable place of worship was obtained in one of the streets leading from San Francisco Street. Since then the congregation has increased greatly, and the church has been removed to a larger building. All this has been done without any assistance from home.

The Methodist Chapel, close by, whose worthy and energetic minister has been enabled almost entirely by funds from the States to rebuild it and make it a handsome structure, with school-house, chapel, printing-offices, and minister's residence, is a striking contrast to its humbler neighbour.

The American Hospital is an institution of which every American has reason to be proud. The ground was presented by a wealthy Mexican (naturalised American), who has charitably given in land and money some 20,000 dollars in an unostentatious manner. It has been liberally supported by the American and English colonies, and is a flourishing, well-managed institution.

The system of burials in Mexico presents a strange spectacle to English eyes. The dead are conveyed to their last resting-place in coffins laid on tramcar hearses made for the purpose by the company. A shrewd undertaker holds the monopoly of burying the remains of the inhabitants of the city, by virtue of a contract with the company from whom he rents the cars, and he has accumulated a large fortune in the business.

The sorrowing relatives and friends are conveyed in special cars, the windows of which are covered with white muslin blinds, the drivers being dressed in mourning with cockades, and the horses used are generally black.

As in other tropical climates, the body must be buried within twenty-four hours of death. This entails much haste and worry on the bereaved ones when they are least fitted to bear it; but it is a sad necessity in the interests of the welfare of mankind. Ladies do not follow funerals; part of the service is read at the house of the bereaved family, the remainder being read at the cemetery while the body is consigned to the earth. No coffins are allowed to be carried into a place of worship. It is the custom whenever a death has occurred in a house to keep one of the great doors closed during six months. In shops and business houses crape bows are nailed over the windows and doors.

At christenings the infant is brought to the church by the commadre and compadre, or godfather and godmother, accompanied by the parents. Hence-

forth the father and godfather address each other as
'compadre,' and the mother and godmother as 'commadre,' and it becomes as sacred a tie between them
as blood-relationship.   The majordomo on an estate
that I visited had no less than eighteen compadres,
and, consequently, could always count upon their
support.

The Christian names are always selected from
the saints of the calendar.   Among the more educated classes the most important saints are selected,
and a common Christian name among the men is
Jesus, or Jesus Maria, which to a Protestant's ear
sounds sacrilegious.   In the same way many of the
streets are named, such as 'Holy Ghost,' 'Jesus,'
'Love of God' streets, or the 'Square of the Imma-
culate Conception,' &c.

The weddings are affairs of great pomp and
ceremony, and to the happy couple, I should think,
very tedious.   The ceremony is generally civil and
religious, although the civil rites are sufficient to
make the marriage legal.   The couple appear before
the proper authorities when the civil ceremony is
performed, after which they separate and return to
their respective homes.   The following day they are
united in the church, which, in fashionable weddings,
is beautifully decorated with flowers, generally white
roses, gardenias, &c.   The brides are, of course, in
white, the material of the dress and the lace used
being of a most costly description, and the bridegroom

is in full evening dress. After a long service, during which the priest asks the bridal couple a number of questions, he places a wedding-ring on the third finger of the bride's right hand and sprinkles them with holy water. A lace veil is then laid over their heads and over this a silver chain, emblem of their being bound together 'till death them do part.' The priest then passes into the hands of the groom a number of gold coins which have been given to him previously by the bridegroom, who gives them to the bride, who in her turn hands them to the priest as a gift from both to the Church. The whole ceremony generally lasts three hours. Afterwards the married couple repair to a photographer, when the bride is photographed in her wedding dress. An old-established photographer in San Francisco Street is the favourite. It is no uncommon thing to see four or five wedding carriages at his door, and he must have a fine collection of photos of the aristocratic brides of Mexico for many years past.

On Ash Wednesday a curious sight presents itself. Before dawn the people are on their way to Mass, and the churches are crowded with devotees awaiting their turn to have the emblem of the holy cross marked with ashes on their foreheads. All day long the streets are filled with the poorer classes bearing this symbol of faith, which is hardly visible on their dusky, dirty faces, and by the afternoon is no longer distinguishable from the other dirty smudges of which the lower orders seem as fond as the Apaches of their paint.

For the general public, Holy Week begins on Good Friday, when mourning is universal. Bells no longer ring, and no carriages are to be seen in the streets. Mass is celebrated, and the churches, in their sombre black decorations, are all crowded with the faithful. All day long Indians may be seen in every direction carrying ludicrous effigies of Judas Iscariot, some of gigantic size, loaded with fireworks which will be burned next day amid wild enthusiasm. The Zocalo is filled with stalls and itinerant sellers, whose stock-in-trade consists of Judas Iscariots of all sizes, and the whole place resounds with the matracas, or rattles of every size and description, which are eagerly bought up. In many churches in the interior huge matracas are used instead of bells, as they were used, according to the legend, in the early days of the Church. In the suburbs and in the interior the Indians are performing their representations of the sacred tragedy. Tacuba, which in the days of the Aztecs rivalled Mexico in splendour, but to-day is nothing but a ruinous village in the outskirts of the city, is *en fête* on Good Friday, for it is here that the principal Passion Play is acted, and extraordinary excitement takes the place of the general sleepiness of the village. On the previous day the tramcars are full of passengers to Tacuba, and thousands are to be seen on their way thither on foot. The pulquerias are full to overflowing, and the consumption of pulque is enormous. ' Enchiladas,' a greasy tortilla sandwich containing ' chiles,' and a number of uninviting-looking compounds and other nasty messes, are sold everywhere, filling the air with a pungent, nauseous smell. An immense crowd of ragged, dirty Indians and half-breeds are eating, drinking, or sleeping amid the cries of the street-sellers ; and the eternal roar of the matracas becomes deafening when the old church clock strikes the hour for the commencement of the ceremony. A couple of hundred yards from the church there is a slight eminence which serves as the Calvary. A number of horsemen appear in the *rôle* of centurions, calling upon the people to attend the mystic ceremony. Indians volunteer to take the different parts, those who are to represent our Lord and Judas Iscariot knowing that theirs is a painful if not dangerous part to perform, for the representative of the latter is most unmercifully treated by the mob, while he who is to represent our Saviour staggers under the heavy cross amid scourging and maledictions. Finally, when the cross is erected, he is hoisted up and lashed to it, while his revilers spit at and pummel him, and a free fight goes on below among them who represent the Christians and the Jews. Indeed, so rough is the treatment which the actor of this part has to suffer, and so mercilessly is he lashed to the cross, that men have been known to die under it.

Altogether it is a most revolting sight, and one

which once witnessed is never forgotten. The blasphemy of the whole thing is rendered, if possible, still more hideous by the frightful yells and execrations of a foul besotted crowd of half-naked savages, whose rags and filth fill the air with an almost overpowering sour smell.

Saturday morning is devoted to the memory of Judas, and a pretty hard time he has of it; the streets are filled with his effigies, hung from the balconies on each side, and as twelve strikes they are burned amid the explosion of their fireworks. The noise is deafening, for not only are these effigies burnt by thousands; from every roof rockets are discharged and pistols are fired, and the air is rent by the hoarse shouts of the populace, scrambling for the coins that are flung to them from the balconies.

On Easter Sunday morning the whole population is astir early to celebrate this great day of rejoicing all over the world.

Then comes the Carnival, a miserable apology for that of Spain and Italy. It is not suitable for a people of melancholy cast of mind. The Pasco in Mexico City at this time is crowded with people of all classes flocking to see the masks, and invariably disappointed, for hardly a dozen will be seen in the whole afternoon, and these are of a coarse, vulgar description. The better classes do not join in the Carnival, except as spectators. At night there are balls at the theatres, the principal one being generally at the Nacional. Here again is the melancholy sight of a number of people met together for enjoyment, but no fun; a hearty laugh never heard, and all the frolics of Carnival conspicuous by their absence. The majority are spectators, and the women in masks are generally loose characters. At about 1 A.M. the liquor that has been imbibed begins to show its effects among the dancers, and from thenceforward it becomes an orgy in which decency is thrown to the winds, frequent quarrels occur with occasional loss of life, and the police have the greatest difficulty in maintaining order. These balls occur several times during Lent, the principal ones being, of course, on Easter Day and Mi-Carême. Altogether they are such sorry spectacles of the seamy side of human nature, that the visitor who attends one from curiosity will not care to repeat the experience.

On All Saints' Day those who mourn lost relatives and friends carry wreaths, crosses, and bouquets of flowers to the cemetery to decorate the tomb of the departed. This custom, so prevalent in Roman Catholic countries, has always seemed to me to be a beautiful one, and the Mexican 'Campos Santos' present a mournful but interesting spectacle on the day set apart by the Church for prayers for the dead.

Christmas Day is marked by the festivities common to all Christian countries.

On New Year's Day the presentation of gifts is

K

the prevailing custom ; and judging from the brilliant appearance of the jewellers' and other stores during the month of December, their sales must be enormous ; and the display in their windows is noteworthy for the artistic taste and beauty of the New Year's presents exhibited.

The little village of Guadalupe, about three miles from the capital, is the scene of the great annual Indian pilgrimage on December 10, the day appointed by the calendar to commemorate the miracle of Our Lady of Guadalupe, the patron saint of Mexico.

The legend runs that on this day the Virgin appeared to a poor Indian, who was on his way to the city to obtain medicine for a sick relative, and ordered him to go to a priest and tell him that a church was to be built on that spot. The Indian, though over-whelmed by the apparition, when it disappeared thought first of his relative, and proceeded on his way to purchase the necessary remedy. On his way back he was again met by the Virgin, who told him that the sick man was cured, and repeated her commands. The invalid was, indeed, cured, and the Indian ran to the priest, to whom he communicated the Virgin's command. The priest disbelieved his story, and told him that some proof of the truth of his assertions was necessary. Again the Indian repaired to the spot and again the Virgin appeared, giving him a bunch of flowers to present to the priest. At the place where the flowers were gathered a stream of water gushed forth, and when the Indian opened the blanket in which he carried the flowers, to give them to the priest, the image of the Virgin appeared miraculously stamped on it. This was sufficient to convince the incredulous priest, who communicated the miracle to his superiors. A handsome stone edifice was afterwards erected to Our Lady of Guadalupe, another church in a circular form being built over the miraculous well, from which numbers of the faithful are always to be seen drinking the holy but very dirty water. Indians flock on foot in their thousands from all parts of the country to the festival of 'Nuestra Señora de Guadalupe,' and the village is so crowded that, on the night preceding the religious ceremony, the square and streets are covered with the sleeping Indians, who lie closely in rows, hardly leaving a pathway between them. The gambling booths and pulque tents are, of course, to be seen everywhere, and do a roaring trade. It is calculated that some 25,000 Indians attend this festival every year.

The Guadalupe church contains a massive railing, from the choir to the altar, of solid silver and of fabulous value, which has ever been jealously guarded by the Indians. The *identical* blanket bearing the imprint of Our Lady of Guadalupe is also carefully preserved.

CHAPTER XIII

Toluca—Morelia—Uruapam coffee—A ride to Patzcuaro—Patzcuaro
lake — A Mexican huerta — Uruapam lacquer-workers — San
Miguel de Allende—Zarape and rebozo-makers—Leon—Aguascalientes—Zacatecas—Lerdo—Chihuahua—El Paso.

WHEN the Central Railroad was opened I decided
upon making a flying trip to New York overland,
stopping at all the places of importance on the line,
or within easy each, including those of the National
Railroad. Starting one morning from the terminus
of the latter line, we soon began to climb the
mountains, reaching at one place a height of
10,000 feet above the level of the sea, where we had
a glorious view of the valley of Mexico, with its lakes
framed in emerald green, and the glittering domes and
flat roofs of the city, nestling among the eucalyptus
trees and its pretty suburbs. After many détours
through some magnificent scenery, we descended into
the valley of Toluca, noted for its rich grazing grounds
and abundant water, and consisting principally of
farms let to Spaniards, who, it is said, often make
enough profits out of them in two or three years to
enable them to purchase the land outright. A few

minutes' run through green meadows, where innu-
merable fat cattle were grazing, brought us into
Toluca station. I spent several days in this clean,
prosperous little town, famous throughout Mexico for
the excellent lager beer it produces, and the pretty
lace made by the women in its neighbourhood.

Morelia is a picturesque old town, full of ancient
churches, with fine façades of sandstone covered with
quaint old carvings, monasteries and nunneries,
whose saintly occupants have long ago been turned
out by the Reform Laws, and handsome public buildings. The cathedral is very fine, overlooking a
plaza, inviting with its cool shade, pleasant gardens,
and trickling fountains, and lending an additional
charm to the grandeur of the sacred edifice, which
is one of the most notable in Mexico for the beauty
of its architecture. One of the principal beauties of
Morelia consists in the number of pretty little plazas
one finds here and there, full of semi-tropical flowers
that grow in picturesque confusion, making the air
sweet with their perfume, and forming an admirable
setting to the old churches, which invariably occupy
one side of the square. The air is delightfully
balmy, the climate being almost semi-tropical; and the
vegetation is luxuriant. It was here that I first tasted
the celebrated Uruapam coffee. No one accustomed to
the chicory mixtures sold in England can form any idea
of the delicacy of a cup of freshly-made unadulterated
Uruapam coffee. Morelia has always been one of

the strongholds of religion, as is proved by the number of churches and religious institutions one sees in every direction, which from their size must have been built to accommodate large numbers, while their richly carved façades and portals and handsome interiors are evidences of the wealth lavished upon them in the olden times. Even to-day it is one of the most bigoted towns in the Republic. It is said that an American was stabbed to death some years ago in the open daylight by a cobbler for having refused to kneel to a passing procession of the Host. After passing several days wandering through the picturesque streets, hunting for curiosities among the little pawnshops, and visiting the fine old buildings, I was advised to visit Uruapam and Patzcuaro. The latter is at a distance of about twenty leagues, Uruapam being fifteen leagues further on the same road. I had a fellow-traveller in a young Englishman, who wished to see something of the interior, away from the beaten track, and we started at four o'clock one morning on a couple of serviceable horses that I had hired, accompanied by a guide, whose brown and wrinkled face told of long exposure to Mexican sun and storms. This was my first experience in a Mexican saddle, but as I had been accustomed to using long stirrup leathers in Spain, I did not feel their inconvenience so much as my friend, who insisted upon having his leathers shortened and riding

English fashion, much to his discomfort in the course of the journey.

After a night's rest at Patzcuaro we set forth on a visit to the lake, distant from the village about a couple of miles. It was a hot, sandy walk; but we were amply repaid for our trouble when we came into view of this beautiful piece of water. We hired a canoe, and were paddled to the Island of Snakes, a rocky little island, half-way across the lake, which well deserved its title, for we could see numbers of these reptiles wriggling through the crevices, or gliding with rapid sinuous motion over the stones, while the water around was fairly alive with moccasins.

Next morning we were again in our saddles before dawn. What a lovely morning it was, and how delightfully fresh was the air, scented by the forests of pine trees through which we passed; and what glorious views we had occasionally of the lake below us! Lake Patzcuaro is said to be the most beautiful in the world; and I can believe it, for I have never seen its match. The English and European lakes cannot be compared to it for grandeur and beauty. It is rather narrow, but of great length, and from its very edge rise lofty cliffs or pine-clad mountains, round the bases of which its waters are often lost to view, while dotted over its surface we counted eleven islands, on several of which were picturesque little villages of grass-thatched bamboo huts. The morning was typically Mexican; the sun shone brightly in a cloudless sky, and on the calm water lay perfect reflections of the mountains and trees on its shores and the islands resting on its bosom, while long narrow canoes skimmed over its surface, vigorously propelled by Indian men and women, sometimes three or four standing paddling in one canoe, their graceful bodies moving in perfect unison. Our journey was, as is usually the case, through an apparently uninhabited country—all the way we saw no human being nor habitation, the only signs of life being an occasional herd of cattle. From first impressions I feared that we should fare poorly in Uruapam, a little village of huts, whose inhabitants had evidently little regard for cleanliness or comfort. The aspect of the inn, and the fonda, or restaurant, to which we were directed, verified my suspicions. When the waitress appeared with our dinner of tortillas and frijoles, my friend, who had been looking forward to an apparition of female loveliness in the shape of a young Indian woman, was rudely undeceived. Although she was certainly young, and not bad-looking, the filthy ragged chemise, which afforded a liberal view of a very dirty throat and neck, the uncombed, matted hair, and dirty hands and face, impressed us so ridiculously, as we called to mind the compliments my fellow-traveller had been laboriously preparing from his slight Spanish vocabulary, that we burst

into a laugh, which did not at all seem to disturb the
young woman's composure, as she dumped the plates
down on the greasy, coffee-stained rag misnamed a
table-cloth. Next day I presented a letter of introduction to a Spanish gentleman, who did a considerable business in coffee, besides owning a large sugar
estate. After the customary cup of coffee, he cour-
teously offered to show us over his huerta,[1] and to
take us to see the Indians making the lacquer-work
for which Uruapam is noted. Mounting our horses,
we accompanied him to the huerta, where he showed
us the coffee, then just ripe, and having a pleasant
taste, not unlike a small cherry; his still, in which
the aguardiente was manufactured from the sugar on
his estate; and, finally, his bath, of which he was
very proud.

Continuing on our road, which lay through little
coffee plantations—our guide explaining that they
were all owned by Indians, who made plenty of
money out of their little plots, owing to the high
appreciation in which the Uruapam coffee is held—
we saw one or two ' trapiches,' or coffee-mills, of the
most primitive description. We crossed a bridge over
a rapid stream of beautiful clear water, that rushed
brawling over the boulders, in which several young
Indians were enjoying their morning bath. After a
short ride we arrived at some huts, outside of which we
found the Indians at work, sitting under the shade of

[1] Garden, or small estate.

the trees, lacquering trays, table-tops, gourds, &c.   I
watched an old man at his work for a long time.
His skill was wonderful.   He had around him a collection of articles in an unfinished state; and he was
then at work on a table-top, upon which the ground
colour, a lustrous black, had already been laid.   His
only tool was a piece of steel, with a fine point at
one end, the other being a sharp chisel with a sloping
edge.   This art, like most others, is confined to
certain families, being handed down from generation
to generation.   Some of the families of the best
workers have died out, and, consequently, the art is
decaying, the colouring not being so artistic, nor the
work as careful in detail as the old specimens, which
are highly prized by the Mexicans.   The method of
preparation of the lacquer has always been a
jealously-guarded secret.   Threats, bribes, and even
torture have been resorted to in vain to extort the
secret.

Next day we left the coffee and sugar plantations
behind us, and were on our way upwards on our
return journey.   In talking with our guide, who was
an entertaining old fellow, conversation turned upon
brigandage.   At the time I am speaking of, the roads
were not as safe as they are now, and it was always
well to maintain a discreet silence at the stopping
places as to one's destination and plans.   Said the
old guide, 'If you were on the watch for brigands,
now, in which direction would you look ?'   I replied

that I should keep a sharp look-out ahead, and on both sides of the road.

'Naturally,' said he ; 'but you omit an important point—the tops of the trees.'

I fancied he was joking; but he went on to say that the brigands often send one of their number to the top of a tree, from which he can obtain the most extensive view, in order to give his companions below warning of the approach of any likely victims. He added, 'I was with a gentleman once on this road when he stopped suddenly, levelled his gun in the air and fired, and down tumbled one of these fellows from a tree some distance ahead of us. His death probably scared his companions, who were, no doubt, hidden near by, for we were not molested, although the incident made us take additional precautions.'

Soon we were again in Morelia, where I parted from my friend, and then proceeded by rail to Celaya, in order to join the Central Railroad at that point, which is the junction of the two lines. Hearing that San Miguel de Allende, at that time the terminus of the main line of the National Road, was well worth a visit, I changed my mind, and, passing through Celaya, arrived in San Miguel de Allende late in the afternoon. It is a pretty, clean, little town, picturesquely perched on the slope of a steep hill, its main street being quite a climb. At the top of the hill is the plaza, on one side of which stands the principal church. This is notable for being one of

the few in the country where the usual style of architecture has been departed from, having been built,
curious to say, from the plans drawn up by a simple
Indian. The design is quite unique, and the effect,
especially when viewed from the foot of the hill, very
imposing. San Miguel de Allende is one of the few
remaining districts in which zarapes and rebozos are
still made by hand; and I was anxious to see their
manufacture.

After some difficulty, I found the house of a zarape-
maker, and was much struck with the patient, pains-
taking manner in which he worked at his simple loom
and his art in blending the colours. He used almost
every colour imaginable, but harmonised them so
admirably that the tints were all toned down in such
a manner as to give the blanket almost the appearance of an Eastern rug. These zarape-makers receive
the wool just as it is shorn, and their families wash,
card, and dye it, and prepare it for the loom. In
making a good zarape every thread is drawn tightly
into its place, the result being an almost waterproof
blanket. I have known as much as 400 dollars paid
for a zarape, which took eleven months to make. It
was really quite a work of art, representing the Emperor Maximilian on horseback. The likeness of the
Emperor was perfect, and the attitude of the horse
very natural.

The process of rebozo-making was very similar,
only the finest hand-made silk being used, but the

hues were more sombre than those of the blankets, the predominating colours being green, blue, and black, with a sprinkling of white.

As Celaya is the junction of two of the most important railroads in the country, it is quite an active, stirring little town, with a strong American element. It has a delightful climate, rather warmer than that of Mexico City, and is considered very healthy. I stopped at a small boarding-house, which was recommended to me as the best in the town, and was treated well. Next morning, after thoroughly enjoying the unexpected treat of a breakfast consisting of hot corn-cakes, with butter and maple syrup, and a *tender* beefsteak, I resumed my journey on the Central Railroad.

On the train I found F——, a young Englishman, whose acquaintance I had made in Mexico City, and was pleased to find that he intended visiting the same places as I did.

Our first stopping-place was Leon, at which station we took the tramway to the town. Judging from the length of the streets leading to the centre, the town seemed of considerable extent, and it is, in fact, one of the most important manufacturing centres of Mexico. Its productions consist of saddles and other leather articles, for the excellence of which it is noted throughout the country. There were evidences of wealth and prosperity in the handsome private buildings and large stores, and the business done here

must be enormous.   Leon supplies Mexico with nearly
all the guaraches, or leather sandals, so generally
worn by the Indians, of which we saw great piles in
every direction; while the yellow boots so much
affected by the Mexicans were to be seen by the thousand in the street and portales.   The supply of saddles
for sale would have sufficed to mount an army of
cavalry.   The whole place was redolent of leather,
and it is one of the most practical, business-like looking towns that I have seen in the interior.

A five hours' journey brought us to Aguascalientes, or Hot Waters, a charming little old town,
with a delightful climate, its quiet streets and
general air of *dolce far niente* forming a contrast with
the bustle of its enterprising neighbour.   We put up
at an hotel kept by an American, and very comfortable it was.   While here we had substantial American
meals and clean, comfortable beds.   The windows
overlook the pretty plaza, the centre of which is a
garden, massed with flowers of every hue, growing in
rank luxuriance, and we enjoyed a moonlight stroll,
listening to the charming band, and admiring the
grand old monument in the centre, rising like a shaft
of white marble from the midst of the trees, whilst
the low hum of the soft Mexican voices, and occasional
ripples of subdued laughter, mingling with the plash
of the fountains, half hidden among the shrubs and
flowers, fell upon our ears.   Aguascalientes, as its
name implies, is noted for its natural hot springs,

which are often recommended by medical men. It is, therefore, quite a place of resort for invalids, as well as for pleasure-seekers.

At Zacatecas the scenery became more interesting as we wound round the road, looking down upon the town below us, while, here and there, close to the track, huge mounds of lead-coloured stuff betokened the presence of the silver mines.

Just as Leon smelt of leather, Zacatecas seemed full of ore. Mining appeared to be the only topic of conversation. All day long trains of mules and donkeys filed along the streets laden with mineral. Zacatecas boasts of a fine plaza and a handsome old church, the interior of which is very fine. There are several good stores, and a considerable commerce is carried on. The population is about 50,000, the greater part of which are miners. The town stands much higher than Mexico City; owing to its elevation and its northern position, the winter, which in the capital cannot be said to exist, is felt pretty severely here, especially during the 'Northers.' The market-place of Zacatecas is well worth a visit on an early morning, when it is always crowded, the stalls and ground heaped with satin-skinned tomatoes, plump water-melons of prodigious size, wrinkled peanuts, luscious grapes, bright red and green chilies, frijoles, maize, salt, &c., while the sellers stand or squat about, troubling themselves little whether people buy their produce or not. They did not forget to ask the

'Gringo' ten times the value of their goods, and listened to his ungrammatical expostulations with a perfectly unmoved countenance.

We continued our journey to Lerdo, round which lies the great cotton-producing country of Northern Mexico. The scenery changed. The brown-stunted grass and straggling shrubs with an occasional nopal tree, which was the only vegetation to enliven the dusty region we had been traversing, gave place to a rich, refreshing green, brightened by little streams ; the dry hot air became moist and balmy, and we were soon rolling through great fields of cotton. From the station, only a rough little jacal, or hut, was to be seen, where a knot of stragglers were squatting on their haunches, smoking cigarettes, or dozing in the shade. An hour's ride in a crazy-looking guayin, or light covered waggon, brought us within sight of a few straggling huts outside Lerdo. It appeared a poverty-stricken, tumble-down village. Our hotel, or rather hovel, was a dismal dirty hole, where we were tortured with gnats and mosquitoes, not to mention fleas and other insects, which I have heard dignified with the aristocratic title of 'Norfolk Howards.'

We found out, however, that the wretched, dirty-looking little town was a commercial centre of considerable importance. There were several large stores, carrying considerable stocks of every conceivable article. On my asking the proprietor of one of them where the purchasers came from, he explained that Lerdo was the only town for many leagues round in which the owners of the haciendas and their *employés* could purchase the simplest articles. But the real business in these stores is making advances on account of the cotton crop to the estate owners and small planters, the business done in this branch during the year amounting to hundreds of thousands of dollars.

From Lerdo we took train to Chihuahua. The cotton fields were soon left behind, and we traversed great prairies in which herds of fat cattle were grazing. Besides being a great mining camp, the State of Chihuahua probably raises more cattle than any other, and a good many large cattle ranches are owned by Englishmen. The climate is much hotter in the summer and colder in the winter than in the capital, severe droughts being sometimes experienced, causing heavy loss to the ranch owners; the great drawback to the State being its defective water supply in the hot summer months.

We now became aware that we were nearing the frontier. We were met at the station by a regular American 'bus,' whose conductor bundled us in with scant ceremony, explaining that every package outside cost twenty-five cents. Almost before we had time to sit down, the driver shouted 'gee up,' and we were off at a brisk trot.

The town, as usual, is some distance from the station, and on reaching the plaza the first sight

that greeted our eyes was a large building bearing
the title 'American Hotel' in huge gilt letters.
Close by was a barber's pole, painted with the
orthodox red and white stripes, and a store, over
which hung the sign 'News Agency.' These things
told us that American enterprise had reached Chihuahua. The stores occupied substantial modern buildings, with plate-glass window fronts, glass swing-doors,
mahogany counters, and carried the most diversified
stock to supply the humble needs of the Indian peon,
and the luxurious tastes of the Americans and other
foreigners of the neighbourhood.

Leaving Chihuahua we steamed off for El Paso.
It was at the end of the rainy season, and the Rio
Grande was, as its name implies, indeed a big
river, for it had carried away the railway bridge.
There was a scramble through heavy mud, stagger-
ing under the weight of our portmanteaus, and we
reached the riverside, where a large flat-bottomed
boat awaited us. In this we were safely ferried
across by means of a stout rope stretched across
the river ; but it was an anxious time, for had the
rope, which seemed strained to the utmost, broken,
we should have inevitably been carried away and
drowned. The feeling while being propelled through
the water across a rushing stream, the broadside
waves of which seem as though threatening to
engulf the boat, is a queer one, causing a dizzy sensation not unlike sea-sickness.

El Paso is a type of American enterprise. Five years before there had not been a decent house, a few mud huts forming the town. When we arrived, there were two or three good hotels, two large railroad stations, and several banks. Every denomination had its place of worship. A handsome town hall, to cost 60,000 dollars, was being built, and, as is the general rule in frontier towns and ' out West,' there was a saloon to every three or four houses. Everything was to be had at the numerous stores, where hundreds of thousands of dollars were turned over annually in wooden sheds that a London greengrocer would despise.

It is now several years since I passed through El Paso, and I have no doubt that during the comparatively short time that has elapsed it has trebled in size and prosperity.

CHAPTER XIV

On my return trip from the States I visited Guadalajara and San Luis Potosi, in those days only to be reached by diligencia from Lagos, which is at about an equal distance between these two cities. On my arrival at this town I learned that the San Luis Potosi coach would not start for two days. The ' Hotel Diligencias,' at which I stopped, was a typical Mexican inn. I secured a corner seat in the diligencia, a most important point, for it is the only place in which one can get any rest during the long tedious journey. The Mexican diligencia is not unlike a French diligence, but about twice as cumbersome and a marvel of strength. By the way, I believe that all these diligencias have been made by Englishmen. The interior has nine seats, three at each end, and three on a bench across the middle from door to door. Occasionally the interior of these vehicles is padded with leather, but so slightly as to afford little protection from the severe bruises caused by the jolts of the coach; and often there is nothing but the bare wood for the unfortunate victims to bump their heads and bodies against. Between the seats there is just sufficient space for the travellers to sit with their knees between the legs of those seated in front of them, so that one is a prisoner until his *vis-à-vis* chooses to move.

As only 25 lb. of luggage is allowed outside free, one dollar being charged for every extra 25 lb. on the roof, everyone puts as much as possible inside. Consequently, though there is barely sitting room, parrot cages, dogs, bandboxes, and bundles of all kinds are carried on the knees, while under the seats boxes and packages are tightly packed. Children in arms not being charged for, each parent has one or two on his or her knee, and by the time the coach is full it is a wonder the sides don't bulge. A full coach has, however, this advantage. You are so tightly wedged that no jolt can do more harm than to bring your head in violent contact with the roof. I once travelled in an empty diligencia and suffered a game of battledore and shuttlecock that I shall not easily forget. When I was not on the floor my head was bumping against the roof, or I was hurled violently against the sides. Whenever possible I prefer being on the outside.

Starting at 4 A.M., we dashed through the streets

at full gallop, and before the limits of the town were reached I had nearly bitten my tongue through, because I had forgotten to keep my mouth shut, and had knocked my head against the top of the window-frame several times. Every jolt brought forth objurgations from the passengers, but it was nothing to what was to come. As we began to descend a steep hill the old coach wheezed and groaned, we were thrown violently from side to side, and a depressing silence fell on the company. Then we came to a part of the road where the dust lay deep, and, as there were no windows, the coach was filled with dust and we had to bury our faces in our handkerchiefs. Of all our sufferings I think this was the worst. The intense heat and the dust caused an insatiable thirst, and there was not a drop of anything to drink. The country through which we jolted was an immense barren stretch, relieved only by the maguey plants and an occasional cactus or tuna tree, while far away beyond were the 'eternal hills.' Finally we reached the half-way house, where we had tortillas and beans, and any amount of pulque. When the wants of the inner man had been supplied, and we had become more accustomed to the eccentric movements of the coach, we became more sociable. The usual theme of conversation, when travelling in the interior—brigandage—was discussed. Marvellous tales were narrated of hairbreadth escapes, owing to the bravery and presence of mind of the narrators. The relative merits of their revolvers were discussed by the passengers, who handled them in a manner which made me almost wish that brigands would attack us, for the risk would have been less.

San Luis Potosi, on our arrival there, was getting ready for the advent of the railway, and its inhabitants were already looking forward sanguinely to railroad communication with the main (Central) line on the one side and Tampico on the other. It contains about eighty thousand inhabitants, and, with Puebla, ranks next to the capital in commercial importance.

It is the distributing centre for a vast area of country, and near by are the celebrated 'Catorce' Mines, which employ a large number of miners. There is a large business done in ixtle, a tough fibre, of which excellent ropes and matting are made, and in hides and goatskins. A merchant doing a considerable trade in these skins told me that the men owning the goats took them up into the hills for six months at a time, borrowing from the traders sufficient money to live on, and always punctually repaying it.

San Luis Potosi was then talking a great deal of what it would do when the railroad came. Now it has two railways, yet when last I visited it I could see no signs of improvement or enterprise, unless the number of new bar-rooms may be attributed to the latter, otherwise the town is much as it was. It is true, there are one or two more hotels, but little can be said in their favour. All the principal German hardware houses had large branches, carrying large stocks of goods, and there were many commodious stores, but none of the display seen in Mexico.

There is nothing particularly interesting to see in San Luis Potosi; and after a couple of days' stay I took coach back to Lagos. I had now before me four days' successive stage, for the day after my arrival in Lagos the Guadalajara coach was due to start.

At Lagos, the night was comfortably spent at an hotel kept by a Frenchman. I took care to be early in my place, and we were soon on our way to Guadalajara.

This time the road was more interesting but much worse to travel over. In one spot the descent was very dangerous, accidents being of frequent occurrence in the rainy season. It was bad enough at the time of our journey, which was just at the beginning of the wet season in that part of the country, and it was wonderful to witness the manner in which the wheeler mules went down on their haunches in their efforts to keep the coach back, although my attention was directed mainly to hanging on to the almost perpendicular roof, on which I had taken a temporary seat. It was with quite a feeling of relief that we rolled through the streets of the town that lay at the foot of the hill, and which during the descent had looked as though a capsize of the coach would inevitably land us on the top of the church tower.

Further on we passed a large field, stuck in the walls of which were a number of little crosses. Here, I was told, during one of the revolutions, over two hundred prisoners were shot down. For each victim a cross had, no doubt, been stuck in the wall after the massacre had taken place. I counted over seventy of these mournful little mementoes of times of civil wars and their attendant horrors, now, happily for Mexico, gone by.

The roads were heavy, and it was not till midnight that wé reached 'La Venta,' the half-way house. We adjourned to supper, which was so nasty that, hungry as we were, we left it almost untouched. The room I had to share with a fellow-passenger was furnished with two dirty truckle beds, a little table, on which stood a wash pan, and a broken chair. After killing half a dozen scorpions on the wall with the back of my hairbrush, I dropped asleep for a couple of hours. By 3 A.M. we were, again in our seats. It was black as pitch, and our way was lighted by torches carried on the roof, which, with their lurid glare, gave an uncanny look to the objects we passed. By this time I had become so accustomed to the lurches and jolts of our coach, that by wedging myself in tightly and holding on to the window-strap, I succeeded in getting another nap, and woke to find it broad day. We lunched at a picturesque little hut, festooned with convolvulus, standing on a gentle eminence, at the foot of which ran a stream, and commanding a beautiful view, which we enjoyed over our post-prandial cigarettes. But there was no time to be lost if we were to reach Guadalajara that day, so we were soon off again. Just as night fell the pole broke, and the men had to go into the woods to cut a fresh one. A dreary wait in the dark ensued, enlivened by brigand tales. At last our men appeared with a rough pole, which they succeeded at length in fixing. We arrived in Guadalajara shortly after midnight.

The air smelt sweet and fresh as I looked out in the morning on to the broad clean street, with its quaint old houses, bright in their colours. I fell in love at first sight with a city, which has justly the reputation of being the most beautiful in the Republic. The only fault to be found is the ruthless manner in which, in the mania for cleanliness, they have whitewashed the rich stone carvings of the beautiful old churches. There are yellow, light brown, pink, light blue, and light green churches! Their glazed domes, of many coloured tiles, flash in the sun, giving a bright effect, which would be charming if one could only forgive the Vandals who had so disfigured the walls and stone ornamentations of the ancient buildings. As usual, the *portales* were the centre of business. There were some fairly good stores, in the windows of which were displayed many

articles of luxury, that gave evidence of the wealth
and taste of the 'Guadalajarenses,' or 'Tapatios,' as
they delight in calling themselves. There are fine
squares laid out with gardens, and the patios of the
houses, paved with red glazed tiles, made in the
adjacent potteries, filled with flowers in quaintly
decorated pots, and bright birdcages, contrast very
favourably with the capital. But the people had the
greatest charm for me. Their faces were animated
(and there was scarcely a plain one among them),
and it was delightful to hear merry laughter, and to
watch the pretty señoritas, as they demurely strolled
along or stopped to admire the contents of a shop-
window. The women of Guadalajara and of Jalapa
are said to be the most beautiful in the whole
country, and they certainly merit the reputation.

The men are nearly all good-looking, and their
pleasant manners and light-hearted ways reminded
me forcibly of southern Spain. I found out afterwards that the inhabitants of Guadalajara and Jalapa
are of Andalusian extraction.

There are fine baths of Agua Azul,[1] so named
from the bluish tint of the water; also a large
open swimming bath. Though the poorest classes
in Mexico are so dirty, those who can afford it enjoy
a bath, and nearly every town of any importance has
its baths of running water, and in many places excellent mineral waters are to be found.

[1] Blue water.

In travelling through different parts of the country I noticed occasionally little dome-shaped constructions of mud by the sides of the Indian huts, and, for a long time, took them to be baking ovens, though I was puzzled to think what they could be used for in this land of tortillas. I was enlightened by a gentleman, who told me they were the ‘ temascales,’ in which, since the times of the Aztecs, the Indians have enjoyed their steam bath, by pouring water on the heated bricks and shutting themselves in to stew. If there is a river near they will often take a plunge into it afterwards ; but there is a good deal of discussion as to whether this is healthy or not.

On Sunday, at the suggestion of a Mexican friend, we took a car to San Pedro, the favourite suburb and holiday resort of the Guadalajara citizens. San Pedro was a charming little place, and I spent the day in watching the merry family parties in the doorways and patios of the pretty houses, and the people bent on enjoying a picnic in the fields around. Wandering next morning through the market-place, and enjoying fresh fruit before my morning meal, I was much struck with the pottery, for which Guadalajara is noted. It is made by the Indians in the little village of Tonalá, a couple of leagues away, up in the mountains. The rude taste they display in the colours and shapes of this pottery attracts the attention of every visitor. A thriving business is done in this pottery, for few tourists leave without carrying away with them bottles or jars, or some of the quaint little sets of human figures, representing groups of men playing at cards, &c., which are very lifelike. There was an old man living here named Panduro, who in any other country would make a fortune. With a piece of stick for sole tool he made a clay bust, the most perfect likeness of the sitter. He would do it equally well from photographs, giving the profile and front face. On one occasion an American gentleman called upon him, saying that he wished his bust made, but as he had to leave next day he could only give him one sitting. Panduro replied that if he would smoke a cigarette with him he need do no more. After a few minutes' chat the American left. But he fancied that someone was following him during the day; it proved to be Panduro, who by this means fixed his features in his memory, and in due time the American received an excellent bust, for which he paid six dollars.

So greatly is Panduro esteemed that the President has asked him to come to the capital to make his bust; but the love of home, so strong in the Mexican bosom, keeps him in his native city.

Taking a carriage, which ran weekly between Guadalajara and Chapala, a town on the border of the lake of that name, I set forth one morning, and, after climbing a hill, from which a grand view of the city and surrounding country was obtained, I reached Chapala.

Chapala lies at the foot of a hill, overlooking the lake, the waters of which lapped the little garden of the inn where I put up. After a supper, with the agreeable addition of a bottle of lager beer, I spent the evening chatting with the pleasant old people who kept the inn, and enjoying the still night as I watched the moonbeams playing on the lake, on which loomed the black shape of the paddle steamer that was to take me to-morrow across its waters.

It was a wonderful old tub, evidently built in the days when shipbuilding was in its infancy, judging from its uncouth shape and old timbers, that creaked at every movement of the paddle. Our voyage took in several villages round the lake. At each stopping place we would land on the little mud jetties to suck a piece of sugar-cane or quaff a festive glass of tequila. At one of these villages a sad accident has since occurred; the crazy old steamer toppled over with her living freight of over two hundred passengers just as she reached the landing-stage, nearly all being drowned.

One heroic American, employed on the Central Railroad, who was on board at the time, succeeded in saving the lives of sixteen by his pluck and great swimming powers.

At one place the captain called my attention to a

spot where the water was bubbling, and told me that at the bottom of the lake there was a petroleum well. Although efforts had been made to utilise it, they had hitherto been unsuccessful.

In the evening we reached our destination, La Barca, where I engaged a guide, and horses to carry me to the camp, just outside the town of La Piedad, from which the Construction train was to start at 4 P.M. next day.

It was one of the hottest rides I have experienced, and when I suggested that we should rest in the shade a little while, my guide asked me, in an impertinent manner, whether I meant to reach La Piedad by 4. I revenged myself by making him ride the rest of the way as fast as his horse could carry him. But I gained nothing, for, at the end of the journey, I think I was the most tired of the two, my horse's motion not being exactly that of a park hack. On arrival, I learned that there would be no Construction train that day, owing to the collapse of a bridge. So I had to hire another carriage to Irapuato, which I reached the following evening.

That evening I took train to Marquez, where a tramcar met us for Guanajuato, another of Mexico's greatest mining centres, and which has produced many millions of dollars' worth of silver. It is one of the most picturesque towns of the country, built at the foot of a steep hill along the sides of a river, over which the houses are built.   This river is used as the town sewer, and, at the time of my visit, was dry, the stench from it being overpowering.   There is a quaint triangular plaza with a pretty garden, and Doña Maria's Hotel, at which I stopped.

In the early morning I scrambled up to the top of the hill and looked down upon the town which it over-hangs.   There were mountains in every direction. On their sides blue hillocks could be distinguished, the dumping grounds of the mines, and away to the right stretched a straight road to the suburban resi-dences, many of which are exceedingly handsome. In the distance, too, the waters of the great presa [1] flashed in the sun.   These presas are invaluable to a country like Mexico, where in some states there is so little water that the streams coming down the moun-tain sides in the rainy season have to be economised by being kept in these artificial lakes.   The presa of Guanajuato is used from time to time to wash away the deposits of sewage in the river-bed during the hot season, but I fancy it cannot be a healthy city. There is a partially-built theatre, which has a curious history.   Several times attempts have been made to finish it ; and when on the eve of completion the whole structure has caved in, though it is said the greatest pains were taken to give it a solid foundation and to build it in the most substantial manner. Guanajuato reminded me very much of Gibraltar, the

----

[1] Deposits of water.

CHURCH DE LA CRUZ, QUERETARO

streets running along on terraces one above the other and communicating with each other by steep little lanes and alleys.

From Guanajuato I took train to Queretaro, the scene of the tragic end of the unfortunate Maximilian, whose tomb I visited. A simple monument enclosed by an iron railing marks Maximilian's last resting-place, and few tourists travelling over the Central Railroad fail to visit it. The Church De la Cruz is also worthy the attention of tourists.

Queretaro is a pretty, dull, little town, the Hercules cotton factory giving what little life it has. This is a very handsome building, situated on a hill, just above the town, reached by tramcars. The cloth produced is of excellent quality and it is considered one of the best manufactories in the country. Queretaro is noted for the opals found in its vicinity. A Mexican gentleman, Señor C., has realised a large fortune by obtaining practically a monopoly of the best mines. Of late years, as the opal became fashionable, stones which before were only worth twenty-five or fifty cents were eagerly bought up for five dollars or even ten dollars, and I have known cases where as much as one hundred dollars has been paid for a fine opal. They are not, however, as fine as the Eastern opals. They lack colour and fire, besides being liable to break, though I have seen some very beautiful stones. Some ingenious person found out a chemical process by which the opal could be made

M

black, the effect being very striking.   For a long time black opals, supposed to be exceedingly rare, fetched high prices until the fraud was discovered.

Leaving Queretaro, a few hours' ride brought me back to Mexico City, and I was once more in the life and bustle of the capital.

CHAPTER XV

WHEN the National Railroad was opened to the frontier, I paid a visit to Saltillo and Monterey, the two principal towns between San Luis Potosi and Laredo, the border town.

Monterey is perhaps the most enterprising and go-ahead town in the Republic. It is a prosperous place, with a beautiful climate though somewhat warm in summer, and has a great future before it. The Monterey and Gulf Railroad have made it their head-quarters, and an immense brewery, large reduction works, and other important industries are being established. Its climate and sulphur springs at Topo Chico make it a favourite place of resort for the Texas people, who always muster in considerable force at the hotel, a comfortable house where good American cooking is the rule.

I had hoped to have found in Saltillo one of the

old zarapes for the manufacture of which it was once so famous, but was disappointed.

I went over the penitentiary and was much interested in the curious coloured baskets made of the ixtle fibre by the convicts. The superintendent was very courteous, and it was evident that his subjects were well and kindly treated. He pointed out to me several men whose term had long since expired, yet they looked upon the penitentiary as their home, and, while they worked in the town, returned to sleep with the utmost regularity. There were also prisoners who, owing to their good conduct, were allowed to go out on parole to work in the town. I was told that none of them had been known to abuse this privilege by attempting to escape.

Saltillo is a town of some importance, being the seat of government of the State; but from all I can see Monterey will soon be far ahead of it in commercial standing.

As we had travelled straight through from Vera Cruz, I was anxious to see some of the principal towns on the Mexican Railroad. On arriving at Apizaco, I took the branch line to Puebla, the scenery of which, though not so grand as that of the main line, is very pretty. On the left towers the Peak of Malinche, so called from its similarity to the profile of the favourite Mistress of Cortes, Malinche, who, according to Prescott's history of the Conquest, was invaluable to him as interpreter among the tribes with which he had to

5841 Puebla north east from the Cathedral

VIEW OF PUEBLA

deal. I watched this mountain as the train wound ound its base for anything like the shape of a woman's head; but, although I am assured by many that it exists, I could not see it.

Just past the picturesque San Diego Mill there is a beautiful cascade, and, further on, we stopped at Santa Ana, named after one of Mexico's greatest generals. From here a tramcar takes the traveller to Ilaxcala, one of the oldest and most interesting towns of the Republic. Here are to be seen many relics of the Conquest, the Ilaxcalans having, it will be remembered, been the most powerful allies of Cortes in his daring enterprise.

The line runs through a lovely valley, fertile and wooded, with running streams in every direction. Away to the right stands ' Old Pope,' as some irreverently call the grand volcanoes of Popocatapetl and Ixtaccihuatl, the latter looking more like a cone, for we are skirting its base, where the head of the ' Woman in White' forms its summit, and on the left in the far distance is our old friend, the sugar-loaf Orizaba. Puebla Valley vies with that of Toluca in beauty, and is pleasant to look at after the thirsty-looking country with its monotonous rows of maguey plants, of which one sees so much on the plateau. Soon the glittering domes and white houses of Puebla come in sight, and the train, after waiting for the engine to be taken from the front and attached behind, is pushed into the station. Puebla is properly called Puebla de los

Angeles, from the legend of its having been built by a monk who had a vision in his sleep in which he was commanded by angels to build it where they had placed a cross. When he awoke the cross was, of course, exactly where he had dreamed he should find it, and, as this was sufficient evidence, the old gentleman set to work and persuaded the people to build the town around the cross. It should have been called the ' Town of Churches,' for there is a church, if not more, in every block, and the faithful have only to step from their doors into their parish church. Unfortunately, these facilities for religion do not appear to have any good effect on the character of the people. The ' Poblano,' or native of Puebla, has, I am told, an unenviable reputation for treachery and falseness. So much is this the case, that anyone coming from Puebla is generally careful to explain that, though he lives there, he is not a native of the city.

The cathedral is, to my mind, the handsomest in the country as regards exterior, with the exception of that of Mexico City. The interior is very fine, the liberal use of Mexican onyx, of which the pulpit, font, &c., are made, greatly enhancing its beauty.

On all sides one sees great improvements of late years, caused by the prospect of three railroads meeting shortly in Puebla—the Mexican, the International, and the Southern. The two latter are erecting handsome stations and extensive workshops. Land is increasing rapidly in value, and, altogether, Puebla is booming. It has a well-deserved reputation of being the cleanest and healthiest city in the Republic. Its buildings are always kept in excellent repair, and its broad, clean streets are a pleasure to look at after those of Mexico City. Many of the old houses are very handsome, their walls being decorated with the beautiful old glazed tiles for which Puebla was once renowned, and which were invariably used in the domes of the Mexican churches. These tiles form sacred pictures, representing saints, &c., and one fine old house close to the Plaza is adorned with several human figures admirably executed in tiles. The building is of dark sandstone, relieved by profuse rich carvings of white stone, and is alone almost worth a visit to Puebla to see. The patios of the houses are carefully kept clean, and are enlivened by flowers. The manufacture of artistic pottery seems to have died out, that made to-day being of an inferior kind. But the clay models one sees in some of the stores in the city are exceedingly lifelike. All the types of the Indians and Mexicans are represented, and the groups of bull-fighters and representations of battle scenes would be worth a high price in Europe. They have, also, the advantage of being strong—a quality lacking in the pottery of Guadalajara, which is only sun-dried, while this is properly baked. These figures are of all sizes, some being less than half an inch in height. Diminutive bull-fights are represented with the greatest accuracy, the tiny figures of the performers and animals being strengthened by wires. I was much pleased with the objects in onyx of all colours, the most delicate being the red and green. Immense quantities are shipped in blocks to the States, where it is largely used in the interior decoration of buildings. As yet no marble factories have succeeded, though several efforts have been made in this direction. All the little articles one sees are made by the humble Indian, many of them being artistic enough to please the most fastidious taste. This onyx is translucent, and, before the introduction of glass, was used for windows in the old churches.

The State of Puebla is immensely rich in agricultural and mineral products. Like many other districts in the country, it is but a step from the temperate to the tropical lands, where all kinds of fruit and precious woods abound. The sulphur baths of the 'Rancho Colorado,' or Red Ranch, so called because the owner lives in a house of that colour, contains some two hundred different mineral springs of various chemical qualities, in which sulphur predominates. These waters have, undoubtedly, great healing properties, and will make the fortune of the lucky proprietor, who, a few years ago, bought the whole ranch for 5,000 dollars, and has already been offered 60,000 dollars for the property. Properly managed, it could be made a most remunerative concern, and, even as the old gentleman runs it, the profits must be very considerable—judging from the large numbers of people who visit it.

The Plaza of Puebla is quite a little park, laid out in pretty gardens, with plenty of comfortable seats and handsome fountains.

A tramway runs out to Cholula, another of Mexico's great cities in the olden times, which has dwindled since the conquest to a little village. Here is the Pyramid of Cholula, one of the principal of these interesting relics of ancient history occasionally met with in Mexico. No one looking at these mounds, covered with grass and trees, presenting the appearance of an ordinary hillock, would imagine that they were solidly built by the Aztecs of old. They are believed to have been used as temples, and burial vaults for the ancient warriors. A cutting made in the Cholula Pyramid by the railroad brought to light a large chamber containing human bones, some idols, vases, and other pieces of pottery. The Pyramid is about 400 feet in height, and on the top there is an old church dedicated to 'Nuestra Señora de los Remedios.' In the village little idols may be picked up representing human heads with features strikingly Egyptian. These idols must have been baked with great care, for they are as hard as stones. They are believed to be the household gods of the Aztecs. Some interesting specimens of obsidian knives and arrow-heads are also occasionally picked up. The knives are thin blades cut from the obsidian cores, which are rarely met with, by some process now unknown. In those days they must have been very clever in fashioning this obsidian, which is nothing but a black volcanic glass, for I have seen masks made from it with the features perfectly delineated. Speaking of antiquities, one of the most curious relics I have come across was of onyx ; it stood about three feet high, and weighed 40 lb. Mr. B., a Mexican archæologist, tells me that, from the peaked crown on the forehead, he thinks it must have been made to represent some king.

With pleasing recollections of my stay in Puebla, I picked my way one morning through the squatting Indian women and babies, and the mob of men, with huge bundles, that always encumber a Mexican railroad station, and took my ticket for Cordoba. What a beautiful road this line to Vera Cruz is ! One never tires of its grand scenery, no matter how often one travels over it, there is always so much to admire. As we descended into the Orizaba Valley, the warm, moist air betokened our approach to the tropical climate, and I was soon shaking hands with the genial traffic superintendent at Orizaba, Mr. S.

Orizaba boasts of two hotels ; but there is only one place to go to, that is the Hotel La Borda. Many travellers will remember this comfortable little house, presided over by the pretty German widow, who kept everything so neat and tidy, dished up such nice little meals and worked so hard for the comfort of her guests, one of whom she has lately married, the leading medical man in Orizaba. It was very pleasant to be lulled to sleep by the soothing sound of the water as it rushed over the little cascade just under the window, and to wake up to look over the clean broad street, with its picturesque one-storeyed houses and overhanging roofs, to the hills beyond, over which the morning mists lay in fantastic shapes, or to watch the women at their washing, below the old-fashioned bridge. Here there is no activity, no bustle—nobody is in a hurry. One would think we were far away from railroad, telegraph, or post. All the streets are swept clean, the houses are bright in their whitewash, that seems as fresh as though it had been laid on yesterday, and the air is delightful. Though life is so tranquil in Orizaba, it is a prosperous town, and there are many fine sugar and coffee plantations around it. One sees no beggars, and there is a general air of well-to-do contentedness about the place. Orizaba has for a long time been the favourite resort of the Vera Cruzans, during the hot months, who divide their patronage between it and Jalapa. It was formerly the capital of the State of Vera Cruz, but the present Governor, having a preference for Jalapa, has transferred the seat of Government to that city.

In company with an English friend from Mexico City, whom I found enjoying the *dolce far niente* of Orizaba with his mother and sister, I set out one day to see the Falls. Our road lay through Indian holdings, in each of which might be seen the picturesque huts of the owners half buried in the shade of the coffee trees. A prettier walk could not be imagined. Under our feet was the soft springy turf, while overhead hung the graceful leaves of the banana, and the thick foliage of the guava, zapote, and other trees, with many orchids, making it a pleasant shady lane. We emerged into a lovely rolling country. Another quarter of an hour's walk brought us to the cascade, which fell from a height of some fifty feet. Its clear waters rushed past us in a broad rapid stream. We sat down in the shade of a big tree, and drank in the beauty of the scene. All around us were the blue mountains, with Orizaba Peak high above them all, enclosing the beautiful valley, darkened here and there by the shadows of the fleecy clouds as they chased each other across the sun, while the subdued sound of the waterfalls, the hum of the insects, and the birds' songs enchanted the ear.

And now for Cordoba, that ideal of the tourist, whose principal thought when leaving the city for a trip on the Mexican railroad is Cordoba and its coffee trees.

It is a pretty town, reached by tramcars, that meet the train and run through the shady streets to drop the passengers at the Diligencia Hotel, where there are plenty of flowers but little comfort. There is a picturesque old Plaza; but the sight to see is the market, where the delicious pine-apples, bananas, and mangoes can be bought for a trifle. Cordoba is noted for its pine-apples and mangoes. They are the finest grown in the country. All round the town are plantations of coffee, many of the dwellers in humble houses in the town being 'hacendados' of great wealth. When the fruit is ripe it is gathered and spread out on mats in the sun to dry; the fruit is then peeled off, leaving the berries, two of which are in each fruit, their flat surface fitting closely together. The most highly prized coffee is the 'Caracolillo,' which is, in fact, a diseased berry, being small and round. There is in reality no difference whatever between this and the ordinary coffee but its shape, which enables it to be roasted more equally, hence its superior flavour. The trees continue to bear fifty or sixty years and require little care.

The climate of Cordoba is almost tropical, and usually healthy, although the air seems moist and heavy. Curiously enough, in the days of yellow fever, or 'vomito,' as it is called, the mortality in Cordoba has been far more than Vera Cruz, which lies 2,000 feet below it. This scourge not only attacks men, but horses and dogs. A friend of mine, who is a great Nimrod, living near Jalapa, once lost nearly all his kennel from the disease.

Continuing my journey, I reached Vera Cruz, and next morning took the train up the line to a point where it was joined by the Jalapa branch. Here I found two little open tramcars awaiting us, each drawn by three mules; and we started off at a hand gallop that was kept up nearly the whole way, necessitating frequent stoppages for relays. All along the road the scenery is one of tropical beauty, and we had an excellent meal at the half-way house, kept by a facetious old Frenchman, who declared that he had already lost five hundred dollars over his restaurant, but (with an expressive shrug of his shoulders) it was such a pleasure to see the guests enjoy the meals he provides, that he could not tear himself away! It was a simple meal, consisting of bobo and turkey, and ending with a cup of café noir. The bobo is the finest fish to be found in the Mexican rivers, and for delicacy of flavour I know no equal to it. We became quite friendly with our jolly host; and it was with difficulty that our driver dragged us away. Pulling down the canvas blinds of the car, we made ourselves as comfortable as the hard seats would allow, and were soon enjoying a siesta, from which we had hardly awakened when we arrived at Jalapa.

'The place to see and die,' as the Mexicans have it; and certainly, beautiful as the climate and scenery of Orizaba is, Jalapa far excels it. A more lovely spot it is hard to imagine. Here, too, is the delightful easy-going tranquil life; for who could be in a hurry in such a climate and with such surroundings? The long low houses in the old-fashioned irregular streets were covered with broad red-tile roofs, that afford protection from rain and sun, and from behind the sun-blinds, flapping over the great* wooden balconies, peeped beautiful fair-haired women, showing that the reputation for beauty earned by the 'Jalapeñas' was well deserved. I noticed how few men there were to be seen, and learned that the proportion of women to men in Jalapa is seven to one. The people one meets in the street are of pleasant, engaging appearance, and the dress of the lower orders is spotlessly clean.

Jalapa, like Orizaba, lies at the foot of mountains that encircle it, the loftiest of which is the 'Cofre de Perote,'[1] so named from a great white rock, like a box in shape, which is seen high up on the mountain standing out boldly against its dark fir-covered slopes. On clear days the Peak of Orizaba is visible.

Before the Interoceanic Railway was extended, accompanied by a friend, I made a trip over the line, which then terminated at Yautepec. Skirting the Lake Texcoco, after a three hours' journey we reached Los Reyes, whence a tramcar took us to Miraflores, the residence of the hospitable R.'s, who had invited us to spend the day with them. Miraflores is one of the greatest cotton mills in the country. The present owner inherited it from his father. The best and most approved machinery is used. Throughout the Republic the 'Miraflores' mark will be found in all the best dry goods stores, showing the high appreciation in which it is held.

[1] Box of Perote.

From Los Reyes we took the train on to Amecameca, a pretty village lying at the foot of Ixtaccihuatl. It stood along one side of the railroad track, while on the other side stood the 'Sacramonte,' or holy hill, one of the favourite Indian shrines to which the Indians flock in their thousands on great religious festivals from all parts of the country. The hill was covered with fine trees, under the shade of which flourished an abundance of beautiful maidenhair ferns. From all points, as the path wound round, there were fine views of the country below, and on the top stood a quaint old church, from which a broad road descended to the foot of the hill. Along the road were little altars, representing the different stations of our Lord's progress. Wondering how many hundreds of thousands of simple Indian pilgrims had worshipped at these little monuments of faith, wearily plodding up the road we had taken, we descended to the inn, and then strolled into the village. In the darkness of the night we saw a sight that I shall never forget. Before us, what seemed the ghost of a woman floated in the air. It was Ixtaccihuatl, nothing of the mountain being visible in the darkness save the snow-clad figure of the woman in white lying in mid-air. The effect in the stillness of the night was startling and impressive.

But we were soon made aware of the proximity of the snow-covered mountain in a more prosaic manner, for the air became cold, and we found that the only covering on our bed at the inn was a sheet and a thin cotton quilt. To sleep with only this protection was out of the question, so we interviewed the proprietor, who regretted he had nothing more to give us, unless, happy thought ! tablecloths would do. We pressed all the tablecloths into service, and, lying down in our clothes, managed to pass the night. 'No more travelling without zarapes,' said I.

Next day we continued our journey to Cuautla. On the way we passed over a spot where a fearful accident took place years ago, owing to the obstinate folly of one man. Some two hundred soldiers were on the train, and on reaching a wooden bridge the engine-driver saw that the supporting beams looked unsafe, and stopped. He told the commanding officer, who ordered him to proceed at once, notwithstanding his remonstrances and assurances that it was impossible for such a heavy train, with a number of goods waggons attached, to cross the bridge in its unsafe condition. The officer gave the driver the alternative of being shot on the spot, or proceeding. So the driver went on. The whole train crashed through the bridge and was precipitated into the torrent below. The cars were piled one on top of another, and the men who were not drowned were burnt to death by the petroleum, of which there was a quantity on the train, becoming ignited. Hardly a soul escaped to tell the tale, and the officer went to his last reckoning with the lives of nearly two hundred victims of his reckless folly to answer for.

The scenery all along the line was pretty, and at a sudden bend we came among sugar-canes. As far as the eye could reach stretched the waving stalks of emerald green, and it was curious to watch the ingenuity displayed in distributing the little streams rushing through the fields in all directions. ' Talk of their not knowing anything of engineering,' an engineer, who has made himself famous in Mexico, said to me once, ' why, these people almost seem to be able to make water go up hill,' and so it really seems. We were soon in Cuautla, in an old-fashioned inn, standing in a diminutive plaza, where geraniums, roses, and violets grew in profuse luxuriance just how and where they pleased. Cuautla is much frequented by sufferers from rheumatism and other complaints, a sulphur spring close by having remarkable medicinal properties.

CHAPTER XVI

EARLY one morning I left my friend Señor G. on a visit to his hacienda, armed with letters to his mayordomos and to one or two friends on the road. ' If you want to see a fine hacienda,' said he, ' go and see mine, but I warn you that you will have to rough it ; you will not find mansions, such as our rich men have on their estates, which they use as country residences, but there are few finer properties in the Republic. Its only drawback lies in its difficulty of access.'

His last words of warning were, ' Mind how you cross the rivers; don't attempt to do so without a guide.' He added that he had covered the distance in two days ; but he urged me not to attempt to do it in less than four, as it was at the worst part of the rainy season, and the roads would be nearly impassable.

My first stopping place was the capital of the district, standing on a high mountain ten leagues distant, so I decided not to press my horse too much, as he was also carrying my baggage. The first part of the road was much as most stage roads are in the interior, and soon I began my long climb, for before reaching the hacienda the whole of the Sierra Madre, which separates the plateau from the lowlands, had to be crossed. Very uncompromising the mountains looked as they rose tier on tier in the distance, and I felt I had a tedious ride before me. A bank of black clouds which I could see slowly rising looked uncommonly like a thunderstorm. I had just time to reach a village before a tropical shower fell. I stopped at the only store, and there passed the afternoon seated on the counter, endeavouring to find some topic of conversation interesting to the owner. Finding my efforts unavailing, I had to content myself with watching the rain as it fell, and, as the storm showed no signs of abatement, I made up my mind to stop there for the night. I was invited to share the family apartment, but politely declined from motives of delicacy, and with an instinctive feeling that the store counter, though hard, would probably be more free from insects. The night before I had spent on a plank in a little out-of-the-way railroad station, and the previous day my bones had rattled in the diligencia, so that I hoped to enjoy the sleep of the just; but it was not to be. The rats and the mice had the best of it, and as my lungs had no effect in stopping their scampers over me, I lit my tallow candle and fell to counting the bottles on the dirty shelves, and speculating as to their contents. Sleep came at last, and next morning after a cup of a beverage, misnamed coffee, I started again. The thunderstorm had made the air delightfully fresh; fleecy clouds hung half way down the mountains, the tops of which stood out clear against a blue sky, lit up by the rays of the morning sun. Slowly my surefooted nag paced along with all the circumspection of an experienced mountaineer, and gradually the character of the ground changed, becoming quite heavy in parts. Here and there as we reached an eminence there was a glorious view of hill and dale, rolling land, and plateau, looking in the distance as level as a billiard board, from the edge of one of which a beautiful waterfall, in a horseshoe shape, emptied its waters in a white seething mass into the river below. The road had now become a bridle-path, which wound its tortuous way upwards, sometimes so rough that, while my horse's hind quarters were almost buried in mud, he had to scramble over a huge boulder before him. Finally I reached Huauchinango and sought the house of Señor H., to whom I had a letter of introduction.

Señor H. was a little old Indian gentleman, how old I should be afraid to guess, for they are famous for their longevity in these parts, the only outward evidences of age being a few grey hairs and a good many wrinkles. The old gentleman, after getting his daughter to read to him my letter of introduction, came out and welcomed me to his house, ' which was mine,' told me where to put up my horse, gave me some maize for the animal's feed, and led me into my room, which contained only a few articles of dilapidated furniture.

From my door I looked on to the garden, and passing out into the cool evening air, through a pretty corridor gay with birds and orchids, found myself in the midst of an abundance of roses and geraniums, fuchsias, and other flowers ; but, like all gardens that I have seen in the country, there was no lawn nor gravel paths, and no attempt at system. The perfume of the flowers was very sweet ; but what excited my admiration most were the azaleas, camellias, and gardenias. They stood in tubs along the outside of the corridor, some of them trees at least 15 feet high, completely covered with blossoms. What a fortune, thought I, would these be to a London florist ! I was told that some of these trees were twenty-five years old. I took my supper and breakfast the next morning at the principal *fonda*, or inn, of the town. These two meals, being nasty and dear, were quite sufficient of themselves to urge me forward on my journey. So, accompanied by an Indian guide, I set off for my next stopping-place.

I was soon climbing and descending one mountain after another, along a winding path, barely three feet wide, in some places ploughing through mud, in which guide and beast were up to their knees; in others, descending a succession of steps, formed of huge blocks of stone, where the intelligent animal would pause to select the safest stone to step on, or sliding down several feet in greasy mud, while far below lay the green valleys and on all sides hills and mountains. It was a monotonous and dangerous ride, for in many places a slip or a stumble would have been fatal. I had to be on the alert for the sounds of a coming mule train, or the cry of ' Toros,' which the cowboys shout, to give warning of the approach of a herd of bulls, when the widest spot had to be selected, in which to await them, and care taken to keep on the inner side, or we should be inevitably pushed over. The mules and horses know this by instinct, and each endeavours to ' take the wall ' of the coming party. When a herd of bulls came along one ran the risk of being crushed against the mountain side, while the cowboys made frantic endeavours to get the animals past, a task which sometimes took more than an hour. My final descent for the day was the most trying part of the journey. For over an hour we were descending, the path becoming steeper and the mud more treacherous until we reached our stopping-place. There was evidently some great excitement in the village, for all its inhabitants were abroad and many curious eyes watched the ' Gringo ' as he passed through the crowded streets. Here I had a letter to Señor C., the principal storekeeper, and I presented it,

with considerable misgivings, to a surly-looking young
man at the counter, who, leisurely opening it, perused
its contents several times (or I may wrong him, perhaps he could not read) and went into an inner room.
I was relieved to find that the person to whom the
letter was addressed was a jolly-looking portly old
man, with snow-white hair, who appeared shortly and
welcomed me so heartily that I felt he must be a
foreigner.   I was right in my conjecture, for he
proved to be an Italian who had lived all his life in
Mexico, having married a Mexican woman.   Taking
me into a little dining-room, he called for some food,
and I was soon busy with a good meal, while he
plied me with questions as to how my friend and his
family were, where I had come from, and where I was
going to, what my plans were, &c.   Then he placed a
bottle of Catalan wine before me, which I thoroughly
enjoyed, and a delicious cup of chocolate concluded
the meal.   This was far from what I had expected,
and my heart warmed to my hospitable host.   Long
may he live in peace and prosperity as the best-hearted
old fellow I have met in my travels in the country!   I
was shown into a bedroom, clean and neatly furnished,
and I enjoyed a siesta after my 12-league ride.   I
was awakened by a sharp clap of thunder, and groping
my way into the store I found my host absorbed in a
game of cards on the counter with several others.   So
I passed into the square at the corner of which the
shop stood.

It was September 16, the great day on which Mexico commemorates the declaration of her independence, and, evidently, there was to have been a great *festa*. But the streets were almost deserted, rain fell in torrents, and everything looked as though this *festa* would be spoiled, as it often is, falling as it does at the fag end of the rains.

Finally, the storm passed off; and then the inhabitants of the square appeared at their doors with a plentiful supply of little red, white, and green coloured paper lanterns, representing the national colours. These were hung on the pillars of the portales, the big wooden balcony of the Ayuntamiento [1] being covered with them. The effect was quite pretty. But they were no sooner up than it began to rain again ; however, the authorities were not to be daunted, and the band in the balcony began to play. I have said, I think, elsewhere that the Mexicans are excellent judges of music, but, though all natives are fond of it, one often hears poor music in the interior. The bandmaster had either no idea of the most rudimentary principles of time, or no command over his band, for it sounded much like a general race to see who should come in first; while the big drum broke out occasionally into a volley, that for several moments completely drowned all other sounds.

The fireworks consisted simply of rockets, which were every now and then fired, after much deliberation,

[1] Town Hall.

at the stone fountain in the middle of the Plaza. Meanwhile the spectators squatted under the shelter of their doorways, or the portales, and looked solemnly on, evidently taking it all as a matter of course, and not exhibiting the slightest sign of enthusiasm. My host's family apparently had quite a number of lady visitors, for there was a goodly party of matrons and maidens seated at his door, no doubt discussing the latest tit-bits of scandal, judging from the whisperings and meaning looks, followed by an occasional titter. The card-players within did not allow the festivities to disturb their attention in the least. From the subdued excitement one might have thought the stakes were high, and it is quite possible that the innocent coppers which passed from hand to hand may have represented dollars. It was not *comme il faut* to address the ladies, and I hardly cared to talk to the few dirty Indians at my side, so that the whole thing soon became monotonous. I retired to rest, awaking now and then under the impression that the place was being bombarded, to find that the big drum was again indulging in an outburst of enthusiasm.

Next morning my host kindly called on the ' President,' who gave him a written order to his colleague at my next stopping-place for a guide to be furnished for me thence. I have since found that whenever there is any difficulty in obtaining a guide, an appeal to the President has at once the desired result. He orders a man to accompany the traveller, telling him it is a 'correo,' or mail, and as this is a Government matter the man rarely refuses. In every small town or village there are two chief officials, the President and the Juez, who are little short of despots among their humble subjects. The President represents the Government, and the Juez or judge settles all small legal matters, those of any importance being remitted to the Jefe Politico at the capital of the State.

The road from here was one of almost continuous descent, which gives far more fatigue than ascending, and requires more constant attention. As usual, there was nothing to relieve the monotony save an occasional mule train; for hours not a human being would be met, nor a single house be seen. I reached San Pedro, at which I was to spend the night, late in the afternoon. It was a little collection of huts scattered over a hillside. I stopped at the store, a tumble-down looking affair, the owner of which gruffly told me to unsaddle my horse and tie him up. During the whole ride of some fifteen leagues I had not been able to get a meal, and felt ravenous. On asking for the fonda, I was directed to a hut higher up. This, from the remains of a carcase hanging before the door, evidently belonged to the local butcher. It is difficult to imagine anything more repulsive than the appearance and smell of this filthy hovel. Its blackened roof and walls, and its mud-

floor, almost covered with hides and offal, the vacant
spots being so encumbered with children, pigs, and
poultry, that the man and his wife could hardly pick
their way; the putrefying meat hanging from the
roof, and the sickening smell, combined to make it as
uninviting a dining place as it has been my lot to
come across.   The owner of the fonda was a pale,
delicate-looking man, who evidently stood much in
awe of his wife, a huge slatternly creature, for he
answered no questions without first deferentially
referring to her; the replies he received were always
short and to the point, given in a contemptuous tone
of voice.   On my asking the man when I could have
something to eat, she replied for him, 'Quien sabe?'[1]
I asked if something could not be got ready at once,
and her reply was simply ' No hay.'[2]   There was nothing for it, therefore, but to await her good pleasure;
and, as rain was falling heavily, I had to sit by my
friend, the tipsy Indian, on the bench outside, under
the narrow projecting thatch, keeping at a respectful
distance the pigs and dogs that swarmed around.
The question of my night's lodging was a difficult
problem to solve.   To sleep in the dirty store or in
the stinking butcher's shop was out of the question. I
would have far rather slept in the rain.   Finally, I
selected the carpenter's shed, where I chose a broad
plank for a bed, and placed my saddle and baggage.
I bought some maize at the store, and asked for some-

[1] 'Who knows?'   [2] 'There is none.'

thing from which to feed my horse. The reply was, 'No hay.' So, without asking permission, I took the first basket I could find, and placing it on a bench, watched my horse feed, while I kicked off the pigs that were fighting around in their efforts to overturn the basket. After securing my horse for the night, I returned to the fonda for my supper. The smell of the mess that was placed before me was sufficient, and I at once threw it to the dogs, contenting myself with tortillas, washing my meal down with some muddy water. Sleep was out of the question that night. What with the combined noises of the pigs, dogs, bulls, and cocks, I never heard in my life such an infernal racket. I bade adieu to San Pedro, devoutly hoping that ill-fortune might never cause me to spend the night there again.

As the descent continued the air became warmer, and the vegetation changed. The fir forests of the mountains were left behind, and great trees of tropical growth took their place. Occasional glimpses could be had of the river I had to cross, passing through a fertile valley of russet-brown maize plots, sugar fields, coffee plantations, and broad expanses of rich grazing grounds, alternating with woods, cane brakes, and banana plantations, while the winding river gleamed in the sun. It was a beautiful sight, and the morning air was delightful, so I quickly forgot my night's troubles. At noon we stopped at a hut to ascertain whether the stream below was ford-

able. A pleasant-faced, clean-looking woman answered our inquiries and informed us that there was
no danger. I asked if she could give us a tortilla,
for I was famished, it having been impossible to get
any breakfast at San Pedro. She invited me into
the house, where I was soon enjoying a repast of
fried bacon and maize tamales, with a refreshing cup
of cinnamon tea. This was the first time I had
tasted these tamales, which consisted of maize leaves
stuffed with corn, baked brown, and are very good.
Seeing an orange tree, I asked for a few oranges, and
was told I might knock as many down as I pleased, a
permission of which I gladly availed myself.

I was then taken to a spot from which I could
see the stream, and they told me it was often far
more dangerous than the river. Only a week before
a Mexican had attempted to cross it with his wife;
but while the lady got safely across, the unfortunate
husband, who was carrying a large amount in dollars
in his saddle-bags, was overwhelmed by the current
and carried away. My guide now declared he did
not know this stream, but I succeeded in finding a
man who could take us to the ford. We reached the
other side with little trouble, though the current was
running very fast. After a couple of hours' ride we
came to the river, and here the guide refused to go
any further. He soon altered his decision when I
told him that unless he accompanied me to my destination, as agreed, he would not receive a cent. The

men in the canoe refused to tow my horse across, as the current was too strong. Here was a predicament! My guide would not take the animal across, and I hardly cared to risk it myself, for I had no knowledge of the river, which was fully 150 feet across, and ran with great force. At last I had to agree to the price of a man who offered to do it for one dollar fifty cents, alleging as an excuse for the price that it was a dangerous task. Imagine my disgust afterwards, as I watched him crossing with some anxiety, when I found that he had taken the animal a little way down the stream to a ford, for the water was hardly breast high except in one place, where he had to swim a few yards! When paying the man I told him, ironically, to go home and give a 'baile,'[1] but not to get too drunk on his easily-acquired wealth, for he had probably made more in ten minutes than he ever hoped to earn in a week.

The heat now became intense, for we were in the Tropics, in the hottest part of the day. I heartily wished I had brought away with me more oranges. For a couple of leagues our path lay along the banks of the river, nothing but stones and boulders, over which rapid progress was impossible, and here I had my first experience of Mexican tropical insects.

I had heard the tale of the Texas mosquitoes, which are said to divide the twenty-four hours into two watches, that their victims may be properly

---

[1] Dance.

looked after day and night. As diminutive black fiends swarmed around me, settling on my neck, face, and hands, I began to think that the same custom prevailed here. Wherever they settled they set to work at once, without any preliminaries; and a drop of blood immediately appeared. By the time I had got away from the river banks my face and hands were bathed in blood, and covered with little red pimples that were irritable for weeks. Three months afterwards there were still some tiny black specks to be seen as a memento.

A steep ascent brought me to my last halting-place, the old church of the little town looking very picturesque perched on the top of the hill. During our ascent we passed numbers of tree ferns, and I think nothing can exceed them in graceful beauty. Here, too, I noticed the wayside crosses had flowers hung over them or laid at their base. One, made of wood with its bark, and decorated with ferns and flowers, looked quite like a church decoration at home. One large cross forcibly called to mind the beautiful words, 'I am the Resurrection and the Life,' for the green wood had sprouted and graceful little branches overshadowed it. These wayside crosses one frequently meets with in Spain and Mexico, where life is often so recklessly taken. They could tell of many a tragedy, where man has killed man in fair fight, or by a treacherous stab or bullet, to satisfy some old grudge, or, may be, for the sake of a dollar or two; or some poor wayfarer may have laid him down to die by the roadside, to be buried, far from home and friends, by the next passer-by. *Requiescat in pace!*

Just as the first drops of a heavy shower fell, I drew rein at what appeared to be the principal store of the town. Here an animated game of 'Monte'[1] was in progress; and I am inclined to think that many of these small storekeepers add largely to their revenues by pandering to the gambling propensities of their customers. I strolled up to the old church, standing on a piece of ground that had evidently been a cemetery, for there were a few tombs, the inscriptions on which were effaced by age; and at the further end stood a long low building, which I rightly conjectured to be the padre's house, built on the edge of a rock, with a clear descent of some seventy feet, and overhanging part of the village. From here there was to be seen a beautiful panorama, on the one side a vast tableland covered with forest, and on the other the hills and mountains, over which I had been climbing for the last four days, much resembling in appearance the waves of a choppy Channel sea.

At the door of the neat building two or three young men were standing, who told me the padre was out. They were the masters of the little school which

---

[1] A favourite Spanish game of cards, of which gamblers are very fond.

occupied the centre of the building, and while we were talking, the spare, unclerical-looking form of the priest appeared. He received me with courtesy, and upon my expressing a desire to see the church, fetched a huge key, and led the way across the cemetery to the main entrance, the door of which was opened after much struggling with an ancient lock, from its appearance fully a hundred years old. The interior was a sad ruin. The padre explained that some years ago a fire had only left the four walls and the main altars.

High up in the walls were the frameless windows, through which creepers had forced their way, and over the door could be seen the place where the organ loft had been. Near the altar, on each side, were recesses that had evidently been chapels or robe-rooms, but, save a rude chair, a wardrobe, and a table of plain cedar, nothing was to be seen. The altar was a beautiful piece of old carving, no doubt of cedar, which from its abundance is used almost universally in these parts; and I spent some time in admiring it. It turned out that the priest was a 'compadre' of my friend Señor G.; and the old gentleman took me into his clean little room, where I satisfied his inquiries as to our mutual friend's welfare. I expressed my surprise at the size of his church, which could have held a congregation of two thousand people, in comparison to the town. The town had, he said, greatly decayed during his residence of twenty years, and there was no doubt

that at one time it had been a place of some importance. ' Besides,' he added, ' my parish is a large one,
and consists of some four thousand souls, including
all the villages and haciendas in a radius of ten
leagues, this being the only church in this district.
Of course I cannot visit the different villages often,
for it is nearly all hard riding; and I am old, and suffer
from rheumatism severely.' I pitied him, in his
poverty and old age, with the responsibility of such a
large area, and learned afterwards that he possesses a
fortune of some 10,000 dollars, owning nearly all the
houses in the plaza of an adjoining small town. But
it seems that most of his income is devoted to
charities and the needs of a number of relatives,
while he denies himself every comfort.

I accepted his invitation to join him in his humble
repast. On my return to the store I was told by the
owner that he could not give me a bed. While
debating as to what I should do, a neatly-dressed
man invited me to sleep at his house, adding that as
a ' baile' was to be given that night in the town hall,
I should be very welcome if I liked to accompany
him. This I did not care to do, as I felt the need of
a good night's rest, and, after much stumbling and
slipping in the dark, we reached this gentleman's
residence. It proved to be a small bamboo hut; and,
as we entered, two women hastily arose from their
beds, and I found, to my annoyance, that in this one-
roomed hut lived father and mother, daughter and

son-in-law, and three children, one of whom was a girl of quite fourteen years of age, besides the usual complement of dogs and poultry.

Had it not been for the heavy rain that was falling I should have beaten a hasty retreat; besides, it was too late to hope to find a bed anywhere. I laid down on the bed, given to me as an honoured guest, my host and his wife insisting on sleeping on their petate on the ground, and endeavoured to sleep, but for a long time it was impossible. They sat discussing whether they should go to the baile or not, and were joined by the son-in-law, a fine stalwart young fellow, who came in carrying a pigskin of aguardiente. I heard him complain of the luck of some people in this world. 'There is Philomeno,' said he, 'who has made one dollar fifty cents in a few minutes out of a fool of an Englishman, whom he made believe it was dangerous to take his horse across the river, when the most the greenhorn should have paid was twelve cents.' A general titter went round the family party, and they fell to surmising whether I might be the stupid 'gringo,' and arrived at the natural conclusion that fools and their money were soon parted. At last I was relieved to hear that they had decided on going to the baile, the sole preparation for which consisted in putting on their boots, which is considered in these parts as an outward and visible sign of respectability. I was then left alone with the sleeping children and animals.

Next morning I found that the night's dissipation had left its effect on the townspeople, and not a sign of life was to be seen till the sun was high in the heavens. When the fonda was opened, the sleepy-looking old lady who kept it told me there would be no breakfast for another hour, as all her people were asleep. At last I got some coffee and stale cakes, and left the inhabitants to sleep off their carouse. The President had obtained a guide for me, a sulky-looking individual, who demanded payment in advance, to which I demurred ; but, as the President assured me that it was all right, I agreed to his demands, which were just double what I had been paying hitherto. Possibly the legend of the riverside episode had reached his ears ; at any rate, he would not take less, and no one else could be found.

Once we had descended the steep sides of the hill, our road was fairly level, and here and there I could enjoy the luxury of a trot. Our path lay through a broad lane which I learned was called a ' camino real,' or royal road, as each man in the community has to take his share in keeping the luxuriant vegetation down. Were this neglected for a year it would become a pathless jungle, such as we now had on each side of us. This jungle looked very picturesque from the outside ; but only those who have been in the Tropics can form any idea of how dense and matted the vegetation becomes. Hanging from the top branches of lofty trees to the ground, or from tree to tree, were, what looked like stout ropes, often as thick as a man's wrist, but, in reality, creepers, so pliable as to be impossible to break, which covered the ground and twined among the shoals and undergrowth, forming a tangled mass, which had to be cleared with a machete at every step. Woe to the unfortunate who loses the narrow paths which run through these ' bosques ' as they are called, where the sun rarely penetrates, and which are full of snakes and all kinds of noxious reptiles !

On arriving at a stream, the guide professed his inability to find the ford ; but as I knew this was only an excuse to be allowed to return, I succeeded in getting across somehow, making him go ahead, and, to punish him, kept up a sharp trot the rest of the way, which made him perspire freely. I could hear him muttering curses to himself.

It was a beautiful ride. Sometimes the road skirted a stream in the clear depths of which could be seen the fish darting about, reflecting on its smooth surface the lofty bamboos, bending over with their tapering tips, or shaded by overhanging orchid-trees, to emerge into the brilliant sunshine ; the stream sparkling like burnished silver and dancing with a gentle, rippling sound over the pebbles. At other times we passed through shady spots where the silence was broken by the shrill cries of the golden-headed parrots and gay-plumaged macaws, while humming-birds flitted about, and myriads of gorgeous butterflies disported themselves around us. On each side stood the forest of cedar, rosewood, and india-rubber trees with their network of creepers, an occasional sunbeam that had struggled through the dense foliage dimly lighting up the undergrowth below. Then we passed out into the glare of the midday sun, and over gently undulating pasture-lands, dotted with clumps of trees and occasional cocoa-palms, where horses and cattle peacefully browsed, or rested in the shade ; and near banana groves and smiling maize-plots, their leaves rustling in the breeze, until the barking of dogs denoted that we were approaching the habitation of man.

We had arrived at the first ranch on my friend's estate, and from a tumble-down hut issued Don Paolo, the mayordomo, with whom I had a few minutes' chat, seated on an old petroleum-box, which appeared to be his only article of furniture. In another hour I reached my destination, Rancho Nuevo, or the New Ranch, where was the principal house of the hacienda, which was to be my residence during my stay.

Notwithstanding my friend's warning, I was disappointed at the appearance of Rancho Nuevo house, and a glance at the interior told me that I should indeed have to rough it. It was built of mud, surrounded by a dilapidated bamboo fence, and had three rooms, that in the entre having two large folding-doors at the front and back of the house. The room on the right was the store, while on the left was another shut off by an unfinished partition of sticks.

Pigs and poultry were wandering about at their sweet will, and the whole place was dirty and uncared-for. The roof, in which large gaps showed that it afforded little shelter from the rain, left an open space above the walls; and over the doors were also spaces two feet wide. Ceiling there was none; and, as I lay in my bed, I looked up into the cobweb-covered roof with visions of scorpions and tarantulas dropping on me in my sleep. Of course the ventilation was ample, far too much so, as I found to my cost when the first 'norther' struck us. The house had been made, like all others in this part of the world, without bricks or mortar, nails or screws, bolts or locks. In the furniture wooden pegs supplied the place of nails, and the doors were secured by stout props inside. The floor was of mud. These houses are built very simply and at little expense, the materials required being close at hand.

Stout uprights are driven at equal distances into the earth; the spaces between are filled in with bamboos or sticks, over which mud is thrown until all the chinks are filled up. Across and along the tops of the walls thus formed are thrown beams, projecting from the house to support the roof of zacate, a long dry grass, or dried leaves. Doors and shutters are placed in the spaces left for them in the walls, and the house is complete. Such a thing as a glass window is unknown. To secure the beams, doors, and roof, creepers from the woods, as strong as rope and more durable, are employed. Those living in bamboo

huts of course only require a door, windows being
needless, for they can see all that passes outside
through the interstices of the bamboos.   A well-built
mud-house, if kept in repair, will last forty or fifty
years; but this one had not been well-built.   Behind
the hacienda house stood the casero, or caretaker's
hut, where all the cooking was done.   At the back
was a small maize plot; on one side was the huerta, or
garden, and on the other a corral in which the cowboys were allowed to leave the bulls they were driving
for the night, on payment of a quarter of a real per
head.   The huerta was only a garden in name; it
appeared to have been used as a kind of experimenting-
ground for the growth of cotton, alfalfa, &c., patches
of which could be seen half-buried among weeds.
Curious to say, during the whole time I was in this
fertile estate I never saw a flower, except the orchids
and wild flowers in the woods.   Everything was in
a forlorn, dilapidated state; and I mentally registered
a vow that I would at once set about carrying out my
friend's wishes to have the place set in order.   Early
on the morning after my arrival I set the casero to
work, much to his disgust, to repair the fence in order
to keep the pigs out.   I let him see clearly that during
my stay, at any rate, he was to live in his own hut,
which had a regular clean out.   My first night having
been spent in a ceaseless warfare with the vermin that
swarmed the place, I had the bed taken out and
washed with lemons, the frame rubbed with petroleum,

and the floor thoroughly soaked with an infusion of anona leaves, which is an effectual exterminator of fleas. My great difficulty was with the hens that had been accustomed to lay their eggs and perform their maternal duties in all the corners of the house, the favourite place being beneath the bed, where the dog, a wretched mangy cur, had also his favourite nook for a noonday nap. The dog was quickly disposed of; but any one who has ever watched the patient persistence of a hen to lay her egg in the accustomed place will realise the difficulty of my task in keeping the poultry out. The mending of the roof and the completion of the unfinished partition by covering it with mud occupied some time. I began to find out the nature of the people I had to deal with. Left to themselves by a landlord, who visited them rarely, and then only for a few days, they had become, with hardly a single exception, a thoroughly good-for-nothing lot. A more independent, rude, and utterly ignorant set it has never been my ill fortune to come across. Their habits were filthy, their dress dirty and ragged; they were always drinking and quarrelling among themselves, yet they lost no opportunity of showing that they considered themselves superior to the foreigner, in spite of the fact that not a day passed without one of them coming, whining, for a loan of twenty-five cents, under the plea of their being starving.

It took more than two months to complete the

cleansing and repairing of the hut. Then I began to look over the estate, and had plenty of opportunity to study the manners and habits of these lazy, dirty people. I was much struck with the few wants of the people, and how they existed almost entirely without having to buy anything.

'How is it,' I once asked the mayordomo, that with your woods teeming with deer, wild boar, pheasants, rabbits, and game of every description, the streams that cross the estate in every direction full of fish, and the fruits which grow in such luxuriance around, you people are content to live merely on tortillas and frijoles?' His reply was the usual one, 'Quien sabe?' The reason lay in the utter hopeless indolence of the people. Nature supplies all their wants with a bountiful hand. Their plots of maize give abundant crops, every sowing yielding four to five hundred fold; every year they gather the crop, and for the remaining six months leave the ground to become overrun with weeds. Some few are industrious enough to cultivate the ground thoroughly, and are rewarded with two, and even three, crops in the year. They never think of hoeing or breaking the earth, going occasionally over the ground in a haphazard sort of way to cut down the weeds with their machetes while the maize is young. The woods around supply them with an abundance of bamboo and creepers with which to make their fences, which they are too lazy to keep in repair; and while they dawdle at home, smoking their cigarettes, beneficent Nature is preparing their food. Their coffee, sugar, tobacco, and beans, require as little trouble, growing them, as they do, without caring, so long as there be enough for home consumption.

Their household expenses consist of $1 per annum for rent and $4.50 for taxes, and, beyond their clothes, which could not be scantier or more ragged, they hardly buy anything except aguardiente.

The woods supply them with fuel, while the grass growing around serves to mend their roofs. The horses, cattle, pigs, and poultry wander about the estate day and night, with no shelter beyond that afforded by the trees, and are fed now and then with a little maize ; the cows bring up their young on their milk, which is rarely drawn for domestic purposes ; and the hens rear their broods in the woods, without any attention being paid to them.

It is true the animals occasionally get worms or are killed by tigers ; and birds of prey make havoc among the poultry, but what does it matter so long as some are left?   This is the way they appear to argue.

Their houses are built entirely of materials at hand. Bolts are not required, for there are no thieves ; and if there were, there is nothing to steal. Their cooking utensils consist of one or two pots, made of clay found near.   The tortilla dispenses with the necessity of spoons, and the meat they tear in pieces with their teeth and fingers. Their candles are made by dipping slips of rag into animal fat, while the lard, so plentifully used in cooking, comes from the pigs. For scrubbing purposes they use a root of a fibrous nature. A few fresh-plucked weeds serve as a broom.

Furniture they do not require. The women always squat on the ground, while the men sit on an empty box, or, if they cannot afford such a luxury will lie on the ground or squat on their haunches.

Their bed is a straw mat, and their covering the zarape. They have no fear of doctors' bills, for there are no doctors; and the many medicinal herbs, in the use of which the women are very skilful, supply their remedies.

But there is another and darker side of the question. They grow up ignorant of the simplest rudiments of education; hardly one in a hundred of the people on the estate could read or write. Their religion can hardly be said to exist, except perhaps as a memory of a Mass heard on some rare occasion of their lives, when they happened to be in a town blessed with a church.

CHAPTER XVII

Extent of the hacienda—Our fishing expedition—The San Martin
ranch—Lost in the jungle—A falsetto concert—The Velada—A
baby's funeral—Todos Santos—Our old judge—Machete fighting
—A fight with a black snake—Morality of the people—Visitors
from England.

ROUGHLY speaking, the hacienda is thirty square
leagues in extent. The nearest village, from which
the simplest things, such as a box of matches or a
packet of pins, had to be procured, was eight leagues
off. The nearest post-office was thirty leagues away,
and railroads or diligencia routes were far from this
remote region. The ranch boasted of a single copy
of an advertising almanac, that had been sent by
an enterprising chemist on the coast. My watch
was the only timekeeper of any description in the
whole estate! I found that no one seemed to trouble
themselves about the time of day, nor have I met any
one among the people who would hazard a guess at
the hour from the position of the sun.

One day, whilst engaged in a fishing expedition,
I observed a number of alligators. These curious
reptiles remain motionless for hours together, and as
they much resemble in colour a log of drift wood, pigs,

deer, and even dogs, will approach them without suspicion, paying dearly for their temerity. Some of them are the girth of a man's body, and of great length. As alligator skins are valuable, I asked why they were not often killed, and was told that although $12 apiece had been offered, the people had not cared to accept, as the blood of the alligator causes a painful eruption on the flesh of the person skinning it, unless great care is taken; and few knew how to prepare the hides.

The canoe in which I made the fishing excursion was a ponderous one, dug out of cedar. I got into it, with three other men, to proceed down the river, leaving the rest of the party to prepare the nets. One man stood at the stern paddling, while another stood at the bow on the look-out for fish in order to form some idea of the sport we were likely to have. We came to a narrow bend where a snag projected into the river, which was running very fast, and just as we were clearing it the paddler lost his balance and fell overboard, followed by the man on the look-out. The third jumped in to assist them. For the moment there was a good deal of excitement, and the boat was in great danger of capsizing; but the men managed to scramble on to the craft in safety. From the reports of the man on the look-out there were not many fish to be seen, and we returned to our companions, who had got everything in readiness. One net had been stretched across, kept in its place by a number of tripods formed of sticks tied together, weighted by large stones; and the whole party began the task of taking the other net across the stream. With their trousers tucked up to the loins they waded and swam across with the net, all being expert, powerful swimmers. When the net caught, one of the party would occasionally dive and release it; on one occasion it was caught under a large stone, and for half an hour three men dived together repeatedly, and finally succeeded in releasing it, lifting the stone by their united efforts. The net having been satisfactorily stretched, the fishing began, four men standing in the canoe, and another on a small raft, armed with long bamboos tipped with barbs, which they aimed with great dexterity at the fish in their efforts to break through the net, often bringing a wriggling beauty to the surface. It was amusing to watch the narrow escapes they had sometimes from falling overboard by losing their balance after an unusually vigorous thrust, or an endeavour to recover a spear that had got adrift and was bobbing about in the water from the efforts of a fish to escape from its barb. Meanwhile the other men were guiding the net carefully down the stream in the direction of the fixed one lower down. Many fish escaped by jumping; some of which must have weighed 20 lbs. Sounds of feminine laughter told us that the women of the ranch, who were to follow us with the tortillas, were approaching, and soon they appeared laden with pots and bundles. A big fat fish was sent ashore to be cooked, and we were all glad when the repast was ready. We squatted round the big pot in which our prize had been boiled, and his flesh was excellent. After a nip of aguardiente and a cigarette, all returned to their task; but our fears proved well founded, and there were few fish to be caught. It was growing dusk when the fishing ended, and we hurriedly got in the nets and started homewards. As it soon became dark we had much difficulty in getting through the bush and keeping our path through the grass, which stood breast high. Before we had gone far we heard a thud behind us, and found that the carpenter's fat wife, whom he had mounted on his horse and who had never ridden before, had rolled off, and there was a good deal of merriment at her expense.

The owner of the hacienda is anxious to preserve his river, special licence being necessary for a day's fishing with nets, but occasionally outsiders make a raid with poison or dynamite, and the fish are ruthlessly destroyed by hundreds. The law is very strict on this point, and offenders when caught are sent to jail. The offence is not always committed by those living outside the hacienda; the tenants occasionally try these nefarious practices; but the general feeling of the people is against robbing the owner in this shameful manner, and if an attempt of this kind is witnessed it is reported at once to the mayordomo, the offending parties being sought out

P

and punished. These people form a police among themselves; I am speaking of the half-breeds, for the Indians are too stupid and cowardly.

The hacienda depends entirely on the former for its protection; but, as may be easily imagined, the boundaries of such an extent of land are of great length, and it is almost impossible to keep a watch over the forests and streams, the rocky nature of the ground in some parts, and the dense jungles in others, adding greatly to the difficulty. Occasionally there is a pitched battle between tenants and marauders, in which guns and machetes are freely used. The worst thieves are those who come in search of rubber and chicle, for they go in gangs, and do much damage, killing young tender trees by hacking them, in order to get a few ounces of india-rubber, or chewing-gum, before they arrive at maturity. Another favourite occupation is stealing colmena, a wax deposited at the tops of the trees by wild bees, which is used to make tapers for religious festivals. The Indians are the worst culprits, for they believe that their tapers are not acceptable unless made from wax obtained by their own exertions. For a lump of wax, not worth a real, they will often cut down a fine cedar worth twenty or thirty dollars.

One morning I rode over to the San Martin Ranch, a farm containing the largest number of men on the estate. I found it a more prosperous-looking community than Rancho Nuevo, the houses being neater and cleaner. The people, too, were more careful in their dress; the men's shirts and trousers were clean and neatly patched. Some of the women were quite pretty, and the wife of the mayordomo wore a handsome gold and coral necklace with large hoop earrings to match, of a curious pattern. The mayordomo even wore boots, and appeared to be an independent sort of individual, with a greater idea of his own importance, if possible, than the rest of the people I have met here. He spoke in pitying terms of the people at Rancho Nuevo, whom he seemed to consider a very poor lot; and in this he was not far wrong, though, I dare say, his own people were pretty much the same in general ignorance and dislike for work. From what he told me, a good many of them were Indians, and it was evident that the 'Christians' knew how to make them work. This probably accounted for the general good repair of the houses, which were thatched with leaves; and I was struck by the advantage in point of neatness, of this mode of roofing, over the grass thatches of Rancho Nuevo. In front of his house stood a large, open shed, round which ran seats of split bamboo; and he told me with pride that the tenants of that ranch had made it a place of resort in the evenings.

On my return journey I lost my way. I was hemmed in on all sides by bushes and sturdy creepers, and had nothing with me to cut my way out but a common penknife. For two anxious hours I

P 2

plied the frail weapon, trying to win a race with the rapidly-sinking sun. Happily I won the race ; otherwise I must have been doomed to spend the night in this uncanny spot, amidst noisome creatures of various kinds.

The people at the ranch were much concerned at my absence ; and, when I explained the reason of my late arrival, they congratulated me on my escape, for it appears that natives, even, occasionally get lost in these woods, and are sometimes two or three days finding their way out.

Sitting once in the cool of the evening in the corridor of the ranch-house, I heard what appeared to be the voice of a girl accompanied by a guitar. On my asking the mayordomo what woman was singing, he laughingly replied that it was the carpenter. Recalling the ugly, scarred face of our lame carpenter, I could not help laughing at my mistake, and sent to ask him to come up and sing. We soon had a dozen men around, and I had an opportunity of judging of the mode of singing in these parts. The efforts of the singers to reach a high note in a shrill falsetto were painful to the ear ; but I have noticed that the Mexicans are very fond of making seconds in a duet, and they do so with fair accuracy. The carpenter's falsetto was not bad, and he was indefatigable both with his voice and his guitar. Of all the crowd, only one sang in his natural voice, the mayordomo, who had a nice tenor. But the pleasant feelings evoked by one of his solos were soon dispersed by a wild concerted howl in falsetto of some popular song in which all joined, singing, whistling, and clapping their hands while the guitarist thrummed his instrument with the utmost energy, the whole forming an extraordinary medley of sound. Several of the men whistled well; one performed in this way with such clear full notes that it was hard to believe that they did not come from a flute. They looked very picturesque in the dusk, their white forms dimly discernible, while a cigarette would every now and then light up a brigand-looking face as its owner took a whiff. The casero at my request handed them a bottle of aguardiente, from which they drank to my health, and, saying 'Está u^d servido, Señor,' [1] bade me good-night. So far as I have seen in the country, the women never sing, even to their children, nor do the men, except when accompanied by the guitar. This instrument is played with a mere thrumming on the strings to a monotonous tune with little variations, and ranges in price from 50 cents to 2 or 3 dollars.

I was once invited to attend a velada [2] over the dead body of an infant—a ceremony very much resembling an Irish wake. On my arrival in the evening at the hut I found the space under the broad roof in front of the house filled with a number of men sitting and lying in different attitudes, some chatting and laughing around a log fire, while others, who had

---

[1] 'You are served, sir.'   [2] Watch.

thoughtfully brought their 'petates,' were dozing, enveloped in their zarapes, or carrying on a sleepy conversation.

On entering the hut a curious scene presented itself ; on one side were several men seated on a rough wooden bench, smoking and talking, while two of them were engaged in tuning a guitar and a fiddle. Opposite squatted a number of women and children in picturesque attitudes, patiently and silently awaiting the commencement of the evening's proceedings. At the farther end of the hut, on a small cedar table, with dirty wax tapers stuck round the sides, lay the little corpse covered with a red embroidered cloth, and surrounded by field flowers, its tiny waxen hands closed over its breast grasping a little cross of coloured paper, and an elaborate cap partly concealing the dark hair. Across the table at its head lay the diminutive coffin, while at its feet on either side stood a bottle of aguardiente. Close by swung a little hammock made of a piece of old cloth in which lay a sleeping infant. It was a forcible contrast.

In another corner, seated on the edge of a catre, two women were trying to raise the spirits of the bereaved mother who was lying behind them, screened from the public gaze. In the corner a half-naked Indian man and a woman crooned over the dying embers of a log fire, over which stood a pot, supported by stones. All around in the smoky atmosphere, dimly lit up by the flickering rays of the wax tapers, were the women and children, with their faces half hidden by their rebozos, and the men, as they sat in ragged shirts and trousers tucked up to the knee, their high straw hats drawn over the brows, casting furtive glances at the aguardiente bottles, and howling a weird chorus in shrill falsetto voices, or restlessly moving their legs to the air of lively dance music.

Music and dancing, jokes and laughter, in the presence of death! The father acted as host, and went round with the bottle, from which the women sipped, after a little persuasion, and the men took deep draughts. Presently two little girls, one of whom wore a gown that apparently belonged to her mother, temporarily shortened to her size, began gravely pacing through a kind of minuet, and soon two or three little couples were solemnly dancing on the mud floor. The men were now talking of seeking partners, and were very anxious for me to join; but this was more than I could stand, and, heartily sick of the revolting sight, I left, declining to accept their pressing offers of aguardiente.

Far into the night the weird songs came across the little valley, rising high above the thrumming of the guitar, and, from the frequent calls at the store for aguardiente, I concluded that a long orgie had set in. Next day I learned that they had 'watched,' as is customary, till dawn, the heavy eyes and unsteady gait of many showing the effects of the debauch. In the morning the funeral procession passed to the lively strains of the guitar and fiddle, the musicians at the head, followed by a man carrying on his head the table with the body on it, just as it had lain the previous night, while behind walked a little girl, carrying the tiny coffin, a straggling crowd of men, women, and children bringing up the rear. I followed them to the burial-ground, a desolate spot. My thoughts went sadly back to that dear peaceful village churchyard at home, shaded by great trees, and the grey old church with its ivy-covered tower. What a difference! The little Campo Santo stood on a slight eminence, surrounded by a rough cattle-fence, but no trace could be seen in its coarse grass of the last dwelling-places of those buried there, save one or two little wooden crosses falling to the ground. Just outside had once stood a small chapel, the only vestige of which was a single charred post. It had been burnt down on one occasion, when the owner had set fire to the grass, and no one had taken the trouble to rebuild it. A little hole had been dug in the ground, and on the mound of excavated earth they placed the table. The body was put into the coffin, into which those present dropped a little earth, and some wild flowers we had gathered on the way. Then a painful incident occurred. The coffin appeared to be too shallow, and the father, raising the head of the little corpse, took from under it some flowers, thus bringing it to a proper level. A man stepped forward, and with a bunch of flowers sprinkled the corpse with some holy water from a small phial, muttering the words, 'In the name of the Father, the Son, and the Holy Ghost.' Then the lid was nailed down with a stone for a hammer. Then the feelings of the parents burst forth; the mother wept piteously, while the father stood with his head bowed over the fence. The coffin was lowered into the grave, earth strewn over it by all present, holy water again sprinkled, and the words of Benediction repeated. The cavity was refilled, the earth being pounded down with a heavy stone till it became compact, and, when the grave was filled, the surface was level, not even a mound to show where the little one lay. All this time some of the men were talking and smoking, and I believe that, had I not set the example of standing uncovered, they would not even have removed their hats.

These people have little respect for the dead. On another occasion, when a funeral procession passed the house, those attending it were chatting as though it was an every-day occurrence; and the corpse, wrapped in a sheet, was carried along between two poles.

I found that the greatest feast of the year was All Saints ('Todos Santos'). The poorest will spend every cent he has, or borrow whatever he can get, for what they call 'El dia de las Animas.'[1] The preceding day is called 'El dia de los Angelitos.'[2] Every hut has its altar, consisting of a table, covered

---

[1] The day of souls.   [2] The day of little angels.

with a clean white cloth, over which is an arch of palm leaves, decorated with flowers, the wall behind being adorned with any chromos or prints obtainable of saints and virgins. Some of these altars are prettily and tastefully decorated. Before the altar burn a number of tapers, made of wax, no doubt stolen from my friend's trees, and upon it was placed 'ofrendas,'[1] consisting of fruit, and cakes made in the shape of fish, cows, pigs, &c., and a glass of water. The belief of these poor people is that on the first day, All Saints' Eve, the spirits of the dead children are present for twenty-four hours, and on All Saints' Day, which they also call 'El dia de los grandes,'[2] the souls of departed adults are permitted to revisit the earth. These offerings are made to them, and then eaten by the living. It is customary for the families to send offerings for the altars of their friends, and women and children were to be seen carrying baskets containing gifts of fruit and other eatables. Of course, what with the preparation of the altars, and the two saints' days, a whole week was occupied; and no one thought of doing any work, with the exception of the casero and his wife, who worked night and day, hoping, as they said, to earn enough to live on for the rest of the year, by making buns and rolls for the feast.

The 'Judge' of the place is quite a unique representative of law and order. Like all judges in out-

[1] Offerings.   [2] The day of grown-up people.

lying districts, he was appointed by the President of the town, whether willing or unwilling to serve. He is responsible for the taxes, which he must collect from each tenant. He must settle all disputes, maintain order, and arrest and take to the town-hall (eight leagues away) thieves and evil-doers. For all this responsibility and work he receives no salary nor remuneration whatever! He lives in a hut, as dirty, smoke-begrimed, and as full of fleas as any other on the estate. He is the happy possessor of twenty cows, is always cheerful and smiling, has passed his eighty-fifth year, and has scarcely a grey hair.

The day after 'Todos Santos,' the mayordomo of the San Martin ranch came to invite me to a baile at his house that evening, it being his saint's day. Having left him in my room while I went out on some business, I found on returning, much to my disgust, that my friend had appropriated my bed, on which he lay barefooted, enjoying his siesta. However, in view of the honour he had conferred upon me by inviting me to his baile, I left him to continue his slumbers undisturbed. In the afternoon I rode over, arriving just as the fun was about to commence. In the shed in front of the mayordomo's house a small oil-lamp flickered, and the notes of guitar and fiddle betokened the approach of the orchestra. On arrival they played a short serenade to the host, and took their place on a raised bamboo stand. Many of the men of the party

wore boots, and the toilettes of some of the ladies
were quite extensive, one or two young ladies even
wearing muslin dresses of gay colours. The men, as
usual, mostly wore their white trousers with one leg
or both tucked up to the knee, while those, better acquainted with the customs of polite society, wore them
properly, and even took their hats off when dancing
with their partners. There were about seventy men
standing and sitting around the enclosure, while the
ladies awaited the fitting moment for their appearance in the kitchen of the hostess. The first hour or
so was devoted to singing, the customary chorus of
howls accompanied by the orchestra ; then, apparently
at some mysterious feminine signal, the women filed
in, seating themselves in a row facing the men, and
the dancing began. It was the same kind of dance
as I had seen at the Velada, and I learned that it was
called the 'Huafango.' The step was always the
same, being slower or more lively, accompanied sometimes by tapping of the heels, according to the air
played. The dancers maintained a solemn silence,
keeping their eyes bent on the ground and watching
their partners' steps. When the lady was tired, she
turned her back upon her partner in a most uncere-
monious manner, without a word, and returned to her
seat, which was always kept vacant for her, in the
'ladies' side,' to which no gentlemen were admitted.
I told a man by my side, who turned out to be my
host's brother, and the happy father of three fine

good-looking daughters, that it seemed to me a pretty but rather monotonous dance, and that in my country the men mixed with the women and put their arms round their waists, talking and laughing with them while dancing. He said that such a thing would never do here, for the men would take all kinds of liberties, and a row would result. He little thought that he was giving a foreigner a very poor opinion of his countrymen, who must, indeed, be a poor race of men if they cannot be trusted to speak to, or even sit by a woman at a public dance. However, he showed his confidence in me by adding that if I liked to dance a waltz with one of his daughters he would see if the orchestra could play one. I thanked him for the compliment, and declined ; but he was determined to show me that their education had been more than that received by the rest, who, he told me in confidence, were only ' rancheras,' [1] acquainted solely with country dances, and insisted on having a waltz played, two of his daughters dancing together for our edification ; and they certainly danced gracefully and well.

He then invited me to join him in a drink; and we adjourned to a little table, at which sat the mayordomo's son, a strapping young fellow, with three bottles before him, from which he poured aguardiente, anisette, and jequila into small tumblers, at the expense of the guests. Our enterprising host must have made quite a good thing out of it, for I noticed the

[1] Common country folk.

demand was very brisk, and the bottles had to be continually refilled from huge demijohns.

At 3 A.M. I accepted the offer of a bed, but sleep was impossible, what with the fleas and the noise outside. Once I heard a pistol-shot and jumped up, expecting to witness a row, but it was only a tipsy fellow who had fired in the air.

At daybreak the guests began to drop off; and the ' ball' was over by eight o'clock, when we sat down to a cup of chocolate, over which we discussed things agricultural generally. My host told me the history and fate of a small American colony that had established itself some years ago near the hacienda. It appears that some thirty or forty Americans bought some land, and commenced raising maize and sugar-canes. Not one of them could speak Spanish, but they brought with them a Spanish boy to act as interpreter, who died shortly after their arrival; and, of course, as they knew nothing of the language or customs of the country, they were fleeced in every direction. While their maize was growing they offered a man nine dollars per ' anega' ¹ when it was only worth six dollars. He closed with them at once and supplied them with all they wanted. When they had raised their crop and came to him to sell, they were indignant because he would only pay them the market price. They started a sugar-mill, employing over one hundred men at fifty cents a day, double the

¹ A measure of about 24 quarts.

hire usually paid, and, in the end, they all returned to their country sadder and wiser men, having bought their experience with a good many thousand dollars. Now, had these men been more prudent, and studied the country and language before plunging into expenditure, they would have had fine farms by now, and have been prosperous men. Where these have failed, other Americans have prospered in their farms along the river-banks, and one man has amassed a large fortune in sugar manufacture.

One day a Mexican, who looked like a ranch owner, called and asked to see the mayordomo, whom I sent for. He then informed us that he came with a power of attorney from a firm acting for Mr. G., empowering him to take the management of the estate, and to cut india-rubber and chewing-gum trees, showing a document to that effect. I noticed that while the surname of the proprietor was the same as that of my friend, the Christian name was different. On my pointing this out to him he explained that it was a brother of my friend who owned the land in partnership with him. The mayordomo said that nothing could be done without his master's written sanction. The other asked rather hotly whether we doubted him. Finally, seeing that he was attempting to browbeat the mayordomo, I interposed, telling him that I would write to my friend. Until a reply was received nothing could be done, and he must return. I noticed that his mozo paraded up and down with his carbine, but said nothing, thinking that perhaps this was a custom in that part of the country, when servants accompanied their masters. After they had left, the mayordomo called my attention to it, and said it was a most unusual proceeding. I sent off a courier to my friend, giving him full particulars of the affair, and received from him a reply a few days afterwards, saying that he knew nothing about the man, who must be acting for some other party of the same name owning an hacienda in the neighbourhood.

That same evening we heard that a body of thirty men, armed with Remingtons, were on their way to the woods, headed by this same individual. We hastily set out and collected as many men as possible; there was a general polishing up of guns and revolvers; and the next day some twenty men were collected, awaiting instructions, when we saw a body of horsemen approaching, who proved to be the men we were going to meet.

Their leader alighted, followed by his mozo, and asked what advices we had received. I told him, and then, seeing that his servant was again marching up and down with his rifle, said that I objected strongly to any stranger mounting guard on the estate, and requested that his mozo be told to put down his gun at once. He demurred at first and wished to argue the matter, but, seeing that I was firm, told his man to comply with my request. Had he not done so

there would probably have been bloodshed, for our
men were anxious for a pretext to fight. He expressed
himself as much annoyed at the matter and refused to
stop for the night.   Later on we found out that they
had already been at work cutting the trees, but,
hearing that we were preparing an expedition against
them, they thought it more prudent to come and ask
for permission.   It was well for them they did so, for,
in view of the inferiority of our men both in numbers
and arms, I had taken the precaution the night
before to ask for military assistance from the town,
which was then on its way, and they would have been
inevitably captured and lodged in jail.   As it was,
they had to return empty-handed, and, should their
leader ever meet me on the road, I shall have ' to
keep my eyes skinned,' as the Mexicans have it.

There are many legends of hidden treasures in this
district, and I heard a curious tale from our carpenter
of an adventure he had met with.

When a young man he started with several
others, accompanied by his father, to the Buena
Vista ranch, near the river, where, according to
rumour, a large treasure had been hidden many years
ago, the old gentleman, who owned the hacienda at
the time, having buried his money in a vault during the
times of the revolutions, and disappeared.   They
arrived there at night, and had no sooner begun
excavating than a vast misty form floated down the
river towards them.   It was the spirit of the dead

Q

which guarded the treasure! Scared out of their senses, they fled from the spot; but, after passing round the aguardiente bottle, they plucked up fresh courage, and returned to find that the ghost had disappeared. On recommencing operations a fearful rumbling was heard beneath them like that of an earthquake, and again the vast shade loomed up towards them. This was too much; and the young men took to their heels, and fled as fast as their legs could carry them, leaving the poor old father to follow them as best he could. All this was told with great earnestness, and he added, by way of confirmation, that several attempts had been made by others, who had been scared away by the same apparition and subterranean noises.

Despite the calenturas [1] that are prevalent, and the reckless way in which the men pass days and nights in the rain, sometimes for weeks together, with no protection but their short blankets and cotton shirts and trousers, many reach a great age. Our mayordomo has a grandfather living, hale and hearty, over ninety years of age; and I have been told of many cases of centenarians, one being an old lady, one hundred and twenty years of age, whose physical powers had failed, but whose eyesight was still good. I should not care to vouch for some of the tales of great age that I have heard, but from my own personal experience I can speak of a number of

---

[1] Fever and ague.

wonderfully hearty old men. There was one living at the hacienda house fully eighty years old, who slept every night on his petate in the open corridor. Before dawn he was on his way to his work, felling timber, and never returned till sunset. He smoked any quantity of cigarettes, and enjoyed his glass of aguardiente, but never got drunk, and was much respected by all for his honesty and truthfulness. 'Old Ceferino,' as he was called, thought nothing of a walk to the Coroneles estate and back, a distance of over ten leagues, in the day; and there were few young men who could equal his pace.

Human life is held in little respect here; one constantly hears of deaths from fights with machetes or guns, spoken of quite as a matter of course. I heard a woman at the Judge's house one morning telling how her brother had been killed the day before. She did not seem particularly unhappy about it, and narrated her story in a matter-of-fact manner. It appears that he owed twenty-five cents to another man, who asked him for the money, when a dispute arose in consequence of his not being able to pay it. They fought with machetes; the creditor cut down the debtor with a blow that penetrated his skull, and as his victim lay on the ground in his death agony, deliberately dispatched him with another that, cleaving his breast open, cut his heart in two. And this for the paltry sum of less than one shilling. I was told of another case, showing the delays and uncertainty of the law. A man surprised his wife in the company of another man, who attacked the husband, but was killed by a stab from his opponent's knife. The husband was taken to jail, and at the time the story was related to me, eighteen months after the occurrence, his case had not yet come up for hearing.

Although the mountains and forests swarm with lions, tigers, and snakes, from the deadly coral snake to the boa constrictor, the people on the hacienda are rarely molested. In the months of April and May there are a good many snakes in the long grass; and one day the mayordomo had an adventure which, had it not been for the sagacity of his dog, might have cost him his life. In endeavouring to kill a large black snake it attacked him, and, curiously enough, only aimed at his face. For what seemed to him, as he afterwards told me, upwards of an hour he defended himself, warding off the snake's attack with his hat in one hand, while with his machete in the other he endeavoured to cut it down. At last, utterly exhausted, he called his dog, which attacked the snake and dragged it off, without suffering from the reptile's fangs. Had the snake attacked the man in any other part of the body he must have fallen a victim to its poisonous fangs. The reason of the scarcity of snakes in the vicinity of the ranch lies in the great number of large ants, which will attack and kill any snake, swarming over it in myriads, the only trace left of it being the skin. The armadillo is also the sworn enemy of the snake, and, until I became aware of this, I was quite fond of the flesh of the armadillo, which is delicious when well cooked.

I could not help being struck by the modest demeanour of the girls and women. They always sat apart from the men in all ceremonies, and held little, if any conversation with any but their husbands. I asked our mayordomo how many people were married in the ranch. He told me there were only two married couples, and those only by the church, and consequently not recognised as legally united, the civil marriage being requisite to make a marriage binding. He told me that before he had 'married' his present 'companion' he had been 'married' to the 'companion' of my mozo, and therefore did not like to come to the 'casa grande'[1] very often. I expressed surprise at such a state of affairs, adding that, from all I had seen, the women seemed to be exceedingly modest, and there appeared to be no immorality among them. Upon my asking him whether the women remained faithful to their 'husbands' as a rule, his eyes lit up, and he said, with great earnestness, 'I assure you that any of us finding another man taking liberties with his wife, would either kill him or die in the fight; and what is more, if it were witnessed by any friend of the husband, he would fight to the death to protect the honour of the absent man. If I were at a baile, intoxicated, and any

[1] Principal house of the estate.

man attempted to lead my companion from the baile, any one who knew me would take my part and protect my honour. If I am tired of my companion, or she of me, we go before a judge and he separates us, after which we are both free to marry any one we please.' With this primitive code of honour there appeared to be less immorality than in many more civilised communities.

I had now been on the estate some three months, and was beginning to think of leaving, when I heard that my friend G. had formed a company in England for the purpose of developing the property, and that he was on his way down with two of the directors to show them over the estate.

On their arrival we made expeditions to different parts of the property. The directors expressed themselves delighted with their investment, and well they might. It is difficult to imagine a more beautiful property, and its resources are wonderful. Here cattle, sheep, and pigs are bred, and fattened in an incredibly short time, without care or expense, large profits being realised. Maize, rice, coffee, tobacco, sugar, vanilla, sago, yucca, pepper, cotton, spices, honey, wax, jalap, lemons, oranges, limes, bananas, pomegranates, and many other products are to be found in profusion, while the great woods are full of mahogany, cedar, rosewood, logwood, fustic, india-rubber, chewing-gum, dragon's blood, &c., which alone will yield great profits. The estate also contained well-defined indications of the presence of coal, naphtha, and gold-bearing quartz.

The position of the estate, not far from the port of Tuxpam, and close to the line of a projected railway, must soon enhance its value; and there can be little doubt that these gentlemen will reap the fruits of their enterprise in developing so valuable a property.

Soon after their visit I mounted the trusty nag that had brought me down, and had carried me ever since my arrival; and, after several days' journey on horseback and in trains, found myself on Uncle Sam's territory, where the bustle of American life contrasted forcibly with the peaceful quiet of Rancho Nuevo.

INDEX

R

Spottiswoode & Co. Printers, New-street Square, London